Terror from the Gulf: A Hurricane in Galveston

written by

Martha Tannery Jones

Hendrick-Long Publishing Co.

DALLAS, TEXAS

TERROR FROM THE GULF:
A HURRICANE IN GALVESTON

Hendrick-Long Publishing Company
Dallas, Texas 75225

Library of Congress Cataloging-in-Publication Data
Jones, Martha Tannery.
  Terror from the Gulf: a hurricane in Galveston /
written by Martha Tannery Jones
      p.   cm.
  Summary: In 1900 in Galveston, Texas, twelve-year-old
Charlie, who fears the sea because of a boating accident
that killed his father, overcomes his personal demons to
survive a terrible hurricane.
    ISBN 1-885777-21-3 (hard cover : alk. paper). —
    ISBN 1-885777-23-X (soft cover : alk. paper)
    1. Hurricanes—Texas—Galveston Juvenile fiction.
[1. Hurricanes—Texas—Galveston Fiction. 2. Galveston
(Tex.) Fiction. 3. Fear Fiction.] I. Title
PZ7.J7217Te   1999
[Fic]—DC21   99-14579
                                                  CIP

Cover photograph and all photographs:
Courtesy of the Rosenberg Library, Galveston, Texas

ISBN 1-885777-21-3 (hc)
ISBN 1-885777-23-X (sc)

Cover and Interior Design:
Dianne Nelson, Shadow Canyon Graphics

Printed and Bound in the United States of America

Contents

Dedication

For Johnathan, Samantha, Paige,
Joshua, Mattie, Colin and Rachel

Preface

This book about Charlie Byrd and his family is fiction, but the events I related either did happen to other people, or it was probable that they occurred.

I have used a few real people as characters in the story. Isaac M. Cline was forecast official of the Galveston Weather Bureau, and his brother, Joseph L. Cline, worked there as chief clerk. Edwin N. Ketchum was the police chief. Walter C. Jones was mayor.

Chapter 1

The Fight

Alone on the shore, Charlie Byrd dug a deep hole with his hands. The dripping wet sand at the bottom of the hole felt smooth and cool. He slapped handfuls of sand against the side of his sand castle to form a tower.

"Say, you there with the red hair! Do you need some help?" a voice called.

Another voice joined in. "Yeah, Red Byrd, we'll be glad to lend a hand."

Charlie knew the boys who walked toward him. To Charlie, they were as welcome as a stubborn cow on a streetcar track. Aaron Yates was twelve, the same age as Charlie, but he mostly kept company with his older brother, Billy, and Billy's friend, Jared, both a grade ahead. The three had a reputation for picking on boys who were younger or smaller.

"Why aren't you in the water with everyone else?" Aaron asked Charlie.

"You're always building sand castles or looking for shells while your friends go swimming," Billy said. "Don't you like the water?"

"Maybe we should throw him in so he can find out," suggested Jared.

Charlie had lived his entire twelve years in Galveston, Texas, only seven blocks from the Gulf of Mexico. But for four years now, he had invented excuses to stay out of the water.

"I think we should just help him finish his sand castle," Billy said.

"Let me adjust this tall tower." Aaron leaped on Charlie's tower with both feet.

"And I'll work on the moat," Billy added as he kicked sand in the trench.

Charlie sprang to his feet. He stared up into the gloating faces of the three bullies. He gritted his teeth. He felt a tightness in his throat, and his heart pounded. He squeezed his fingers into his hands and flew into the hecklers with his fists jabbing the air. He managed to land a few light punches before Aaron hit him in the eye. Charlie fell to the ground.

The Yates brothers and their friend ran laughing into the surf.

Charlie got up. He whistled for his dog, Spatter, who chased sea gulls down the beach. He yelled to his twin sister, Maggie. "I'm leaving!"

Maggie called back to him from the water. "Charlie, you should come on in! The waves are really big today."

For a minute, Charlie watched his friends playing in the Gulf water. He listened to their squeals of laughter. A few of the braver boys ventured far out in the rough surf. They jumped breakers until they reached water so deep they couldn't touch bottom.

Maggie and some of the girls hung onto pieces of driftwood or anything that would float and take them back to shore. Many young people seemed content to relax and bob up and down, letting the water's energy carry them westward down the beach.

Charlie heard gray and white sea gulls overhead, fussing and begging for food. Other gulls walked where the waves lapped the shore. He watched them take turns winging out over the water to check for small fish. When one would fly back carrying a fish in its mouth, the rest would squawk in protest and chase it, trying to take the choice morsel for themselves.

"They all gang up against one—just like those boys!" Charlie grumbled. "Why won't those rowdies leave me alone?" He kicked down the rest of the castle and flattened it with his feet. Then he stormed off toward home.

That late afternoon of September 6, 1900, a strong wind blew off the Gulf. It stirred sand into the salty moisture in the air, like a cook stirs sugar into a liquid. The mixture on Charlie's skin felt sticky and gritty.

When he got home, Charlie slammed the front door hard and stomped into the entry hall.

"Charlie, you look as if you're madder than an old wet hen! What happened to your eye? You've been fighting again, haven't you?" his mother asked.

"Some boys jumped on me," he said, hanging his head.

"I wouldn't be surprised if you started it," she said. "What am I going to do with you if you don't learn to control your temper? I thought having a job would settle you down, but it hasn't. Stay in your room the rest of the evening!"

Charlie and Aaron had had other conflicts. One had occurred in the classroom at school. The teacher, Miss Bingham, had instructed her students to copy a poem for their final grades in penmanship. Charlie bent over his work and tried to do his best handwriting. He remembered to touch the pen's point against the side of the inkwell—to prevent dropping a blob of ink on his paper.

As Charlie began the last line of the poem, someone bumped his arm. The jolt caused his pen to make a black mark all the way to the title. Charlie threw the pen down on his paper and looked up at the same time. He saw Aaron Yates, with a self-satisfied grin on his face, taking his own neatly written paper to the teacher's desk.

Charlie jumped from his seat and grabbed Aaron's arm, spinning Aaron around. "You did that on purpose!" Charlie yelled.

The other students watched to see what would happen. Miss Bingham said, "Boys, stop that this minute!"

Charlie didn't stop. He reached out to snatch Aaron's paper out of his hand. Just in time, Aaron raised the paper high over his head where Charlie couldn't reach.

The teacher started toward them and shouted, "I said to stop it!"

Surprising the taller boy, Charlie stepped up on the seat of his desk, jumped, and grabbed the paper. He wadded it into a ball and threw it on the floor at Aaron's feet.

Miss Bingham caught hold of one of Charlie's ears. She twisted it. Charlie cried, "Ouch!"

"You're going to the principal," Miss Bingham said. She pulled Charlie by the ear to the school office.

Charlie explained to the principal how Aaron had intentionally ruined *his* penmanship paper first.

"That is no excuse for taking classroom matters into your own hands," the principal said. "You should have told your teacher. I'm sure she would have allowed you to stay after school to write your poem again. As it is, I'm going to use my paddle and notify your mother."

At the end of the school year, Mama had asked a friend, who worked in the Santa Fe Railroad freight depot, to give her son a summer job. She said to Charlie, "Perhaps, working will help cool your temper and keep you out of trouble during summer vacation."

But Charlie kept his guard up—ready to fight at any time—even when he knew he'd lose.

Charlie ate his supper on a tray in his bedroom. When he finished, he walked over to a front window and looked down. Bright moonlight shone on a well-kept lawn. Palm trees dotted the yard, and pink flowers bloomed on oleander bushes.

Charlie sucked in a quick breath. "He's here again," he groaned.

Across the street, a man unknown to him stood facing the Byrds' home. Charlie had seen the same suspicious person several times during the summer. The man would station himself in approximately the same spot and stare at their house for a brief period. Then he'd leave.

Without considering the consequences, Charlie raced from his bedroom, down the stairs, and out the front door. Before he had time to cross the street to confront the man, the stranger turned and hurried away. Charlie didn't follow him, but he got a good look at him.

The man was thin and stood about five feet ten inches tall. He wore a white long-sleeved shirt, black tie, and trousers held up by black suspenders. Instead of the usual straw hat worn by most men in the summer, he wore a black felt derby pulled down low over his eyes. A full brown beard and a mustache covered most of his face.

Breathing hard, Charlie walked slowly back to his bedroom and closed the door. He sat on his bed. The stranger had first appeared at the beginning of the summer. Always before, Charlie had seen him near sundown or at night on weekends. Now he'd shown up on Thursday.

After seeing him the third time, Charlie had mentioned the man to his mother and sister. They had never seen him, because they seldom noticed what went on in or near the street. Charlie did. His bedroom and the upstairs sitting room faced the front yard.

Mama had laughed, and with a wave of her hand, said, "Charlie, you're imagining things."

Maggie had said, "Be sure and tell me the next time he comes, so I can see him, too."

Charlie knew Maggie liked anything mysterious. But Maggie never seemed to be around when he saw the man. One night, Charlie woke her at ten o'clock. By the time they got from her bedroom at the back of the house, to the window in his room, the man had disappeared.

About the middle of the summer, Charlie and his best friend, Thad, had set a trap to catch the stranger. But their plan had failed.

Friday, September 7, when Charlie came home from his job at the freight depot, Maggie waited for him in the front yard. "Will you go swimming with me this afternoon?" she asked.

"No, I'm playing baseball," he said as he walked into the house.

Charlie called, "I'm home, Mama," and went straight to his bedroom. He flopped down on his bed to rest before the ball game. Maybe he'd hit a home run today.

Maggie came in and begged, "Please, please."

Charlie raised up to sit on the side of the bed. "I won't change my mind, so go on and leave me alone!"

"I'm not leaving until I tell you what I've been thinking," Maggie said. "You see, I know the *real* reason you don't want to go swimming. And it's not because you planned to play baseball."

"It is, too! I told Thad and the fellows I'd meet them about 5:30 at the vacant lot, and if I don't show up, they'll leave me out the next time. You don't believe anything I say."

"I might believe you if you told the truth, but you're lying, Charlie. You make excuses not to go swimming. The truth is, you're afraid of the water!"

"I am not!" Charlie said through gritted teeth. To keep Maggie from seeing his eyes welling up with tears, he bent over to rub his dog Spatter's neck. He saw a fat mosquito land on his ankle. He felt its bite. With a quick slap, Charlie squashed it, smearing the blood from its full belly. He wiped his hand on his pants, but he didn't bother to wipe the blood off his ankle.

"You are, too, scared!" Maggie insisted. "I know your secret. And now, I guess you're going to throw one of your conniption fits—your ears are red."

"I have a right to get mad," Charlie shouted. "You're just like one of those old gulls—always squawking at me!"

He stood up to face Maggie. "Anyway, it's probably going to rain. On my way home from work, I saw a storm warning flag flying from the pole on top of the Levy Building."

Until that moment, Charlie had forgotten about the square red flag with the black square in the center. The weathermen flew the flag to signal they expected a storm. Two flags warned of a hurricane.

"So what if it does rain? We might get wet?" Maggie laughed. She continued to tease him. "We live on the Gulf coast and you're afraid of water! Go on and admit it."

Charlie stomped his foot and yelled, "You know I'm a good swimmer, because Papa C taught us both! Why would you get such an idea in your head?"

The twins had given their father, Cole Byrd, the name, Papa C. As young children, hearing their mother say Cole, they began calling him Papa Cole. They later shortened it to Papa C.

"I know you *used* to be a good swimmer," Maggie said. "But I haven't seen you in water deeper than your ankles in years."

It had been four years since that summer day their father went fishing out in the Gulf with two friends. The men didn't return that night as planned. The next day, their battered boat washed in west of Galveston. The authorities said apparently the boat had been caught in a squall, and all had drowned.

Once more, Charlie lied to his sister. "Well, when I go with the fellows, I swim. You're not always with me." He ducked his head again.

"Then, go with me this evening and prove it," Maggie said. "You know Mama won't let me go by myself late in the day on weekends—too many tourists. And if I go earlier, I end up a solid mass of freckles and sunburn."

Charlie looked at Maggie. They had the same golden-red hair, and their eyes were such a dark brown their pupils didn't show. But he wondered why Maggie worried so much about keeping her skin white. It didn't trouble *him* that freckles covered his face, so close together he couldn't put a finger between them. He figured when he got a few more to fill in the small gaps of white skin, the tan color would be solid. No one would even know he had freckles.

The only thing about his looks that bothered Charlie was his short height. He stood as straight and tall as he could, especially around Maggie. She was about four inches taller than he. Since Charlie had begun to develop muscles, he looked forward to having a muscular build like his father. He believed his father had been as strong as any man in Galveston.

"Not today, Maggie—I can't go with you," Charlie said. "Now, go away!"

Maggie left her brother's bedroom calling, "Mama!"

Next week, I'm going to slip off to the beach early one morning when no one else is there, Charlie vowed to himself. *This time, I'll force myself to go in. I'll show her!*

Charlie and Maggie often knew each other's thoughts—as if they could crawl right into each other's brain and listen. This intrigued Charlie. He wondered if all twins could do the same thing. He couldn't hide anything from Maggie. Now, she knew about his fear of water.

He believed Maggie had also read his mind the night his father brought them the stray dog. Charlie had silently wished he'd found the mutt himself, so he wouldn't have to share him with anyone.

Maggie must have known, because she had said, "I know you want a dog of your very own, so I'm going to give you my half of this one."

The small dog had a bobbed tail, and his spots caused him to look as if he'd been spattered with black paint. So Charlie had named him Spatter.

Charlie followed Maggie to their mother's bedroom.

"Mama," Maggie said again as she burst into the room.

Polly Byrd sat at her sewing machine, but she took her feet off the pedal to stop the needle's action. She pushed back a damp curl, fallen from the blond hair piled high on her head. She turned toward Maggie and Charlie.

"I've been trying to ignore your argument, but I'm about out of patience," she said. "Make it brief. If I don't keep at my sewing, I'll never have this dress finished by six o'clock—the time I told Mrs. Brewster to pick it up."

The twins' mother took in sewing to help support herself and her children. Although she mainly made dresses for ladies, she also decorated hats and did mending. Papa C had left money in the bank, but the extra income came in handy.

Mama had inherited the house she and her children lived in from her parents. The large white two-story home had blue shutters and blue trim around the doors and windows. To protect the house from high water, it stood a little over four feet off the ground on brick pillars. Nine steps led from the ground to a large front gallery, or porch. Above that, a matching gallery served the second floor. Smaller porches graced the back and the east side.

"Mama, it's so hot. All I want is to cool off in the surf, but Charlie refuses to go with me," Maggie pleaded.

"Is that what the argument was all about? I'd take you myself if I could. I'd like a swim—it is hot today," Mama said. "Go with her, Charlie. I'll have supper ready when you two return. Be back by eight o'clock."

"I'm supposed to play baseball," Charlie said.

"Don't act impudent, young man. And I'd better not hear any more squabbling. Now skedaddle out of here, so I can get to work."

With her chin held high, Maggie turned and marched out of the room in front of Charlie. "You have to go," she said, looking back over her shoulder.

"I heard her." Charlie stuck out his tongue.

Maggie laughed, and with a fling of her long red hair, she pranced off down the hall.

Charlie went to his room and slammed the door. He sat on the floor and talked to Spatter. "I used to enjoy swimming in the Gulf of Mexico. I still remember how the waves felt. After a long time in the water, when I'd get out—and even while walking home—I could still feel them pushing me. Now I'm scared to get in even up to my knees."

He shuddered as he relived the last time he went swimming. It had happened soon after his father disappeared. A strong undertow pulled his feet out from under him. Charlie had to struggle to raise his head above water. He came up sputtering and coughing. His throat and nose burned. He had swallowed so much salty water he threw up.

That was when Charlie decided that the sea wanted to take him, too, as it had taken his father.

Later that Friday afternoon, Charlie and Maggie, dressed in their bathing clothes, left the house. Mama had made Maggie's bathing costume from blue alpaca. It sported a below-the-knee length skirt, short puffed sleeves, and a sailor collar trimmed in red and white braid. To complete her outfit, Maggie wore a ruffled cap, black stockings, and shoes.

Charlie wore his one-piece black wool suit with short sleeves and buttons up the front. He went barefoot. He'd gone without shoes all summer except at work, so his feet had gotten tough.

"First, we have to go by the vacant lot," Charlie told Maggie. "I need to tell Thad and the others I won't be able to play baseball. And I plan to let them know it isn't my fault!"

"The sky's overcast," Maggie said. "If there really is a storm coming, the waves should be even bigger than yesterday. We'll have a lot of fun. That is, if you'll get in the water."

As they walked, she sang the first verse and the chorus of "Camptown Races." Charlie clinched his lips tightly. He picked up shells from the oyster-shell-paved street and threw them as hard as he could. He sailed them into the air or bounced them furiously off the street.

"Don't act as if you're so mad you could bite nails," Maggie said. "You'll have a good time if you try."

Charlie hurled another shell down the street. He dreaded the teasing he'd get from the boys—having to miss the game to take his sister to the beach! He hoped he wouldn't run into Aaron Yates. He couldn't stand that boy. And besides, his eye still hurt from yesterday's fight.

Chapter 2

Storm Warnings

The twins didn't find any boys waiting to play baseball at the vacant lot. So they headed back toward the beach. As they hastened down 26th Street, they could see the surf eight blocks away. "Look at those waves!" Maggie said.

"I told you a storm was coming. I knew the water would be too rough for us to swim," Charlie told her.

"I suppose it is, but let's go watch it for awhile anyway," Maggie said.

When Charlie and Maggie got to the shore, they found Thad and some of the other ball players.

"I'm glad you're here," Thad said. "We cancelled the game to come see the high surf. I was about to go to your house to get you."

Charlie's best friend, Thadeus Brickel, was called Thad for short. He lived three blocks north of the Byrds' home and next to the vacant lot where the boys played baseball.

Opposite from Charlie in looks, Thad had blond hair and mischievous blue eyes. He was tall for his age and somewhat chubby. But he and Charlie thought alike. When it came to playing practical jokes on others, what one boy couldn't think of, the other one could.

Charlie, Thad, Maggie, and a few friends stood together barely beyond where the waves crashed onto the beach. They had to yell in order to be heard over the thunderous sound.

"Look at all the land crabs," Thad said, grinning, as the little creatures ran around their feet.

Charlie chuckled at the thought of his and Thad's secret. Both boys wanted to brag about being the ones who played that great trick on their teacher. But they held their tongues, afraid the information might get back to the school principal.

On the last day of school in the spring, Charlie and Thad had gone to school early and filled Miss Bingham's desk drawer with land crabs. When she opened the drawer, she screamed and ran from the room. In the midst of loud laughter and girls' squeals, the crabs skittered in all directions.

Charlie had enjoyed the joke, but he couldn't keep from feeling sorry for the crabs. He figured they felt as frightened and out of place in the school room as *he* did in the ocean.

The principal had come in and made all the boy students catch the crabs and put them into a box. Next, he questioned the boys. When no one had confessed to pulling the prank, he had thrown his hands in the air and said, "Since it's the last day of school, I'll drop the issue. Just don't ever let this happen again."

"I've never seen the waves so high that *no* one was swimming," Charlie said, forgetting about the land crabs.

"It's dangerous out there," Thad exclaimed. "And what a racket those breakers are making!"

"They really look like fun," Maggie shouted. "If the water wasn't so dirty with sand, I'd be tempted to wade out a little way."

An elderly couple walked over to the young people. "Yesterday, my wife and I came from Dallas to spend a week here," the man said.

"We're staying at the Tremont Hotel in town," the woman told them. She strained her voice to be heard over the wind and waves, and she tried in vain to smooth down her hair.

"Galveston is one of our favorite places for a vacation," the man said. "I'm concerned, though, about the storm warning flags we saw today. We wonder if we should leave the island."

"We'll probably only have an overflow. Sometimes, if there's a storm out there, water from the Gulf will flow inland," Charlie explained. "But it always goes back out within a few hours, so we don't worry about it."

"That's why all the houses are built up off the ground—to protect them from overflows," Maggie added.

"I don't know," the man mumbled, as he and his wife walked away. "If there's a storm coming . . ."

Charlie watched the water. He put up a hand to shield his eyes from wind and blowing sand. He breathed in the familiar fishy smell of the sea. He shivered with excitement as well as fear.

Water as far as you can see. And it never stops moving. Over and over, waves keep coming—each one pounds the shore with a roar and a splash—then turns into foam and slides back to sea—to make way for the next one.

Occasionally, Charlie would slip away with Spatter and go to the beach when his friends weren't there. He always intended to get in the water. He'd gaze at the sea, spellbound for awhile. Then, he'd begin to think of his father and his fear would overtake him.

"I see Isaac Cline coming in his buggy," Maggie said.

"I'm going to talk to him," Charlie called as he left his friends.

He ran toward the slim weatherman who wore a

frock coat, stiff white collar, and a necktie beneath his neatly trimmed Van Dyke beard.

As Dr. Cline stepped down from the buggy, he held his broad-brimmed white hat on his head. He stood on the beach and looked up at the sky.

Charlie had always known Dr. Isaac Cline, chief of the Galveston Weather Bureau, and his brother, Joseph, chief clerk for the Bureau. They lived only a few blocks from the Byrds' home. Often, Charlie stopped to chat with the Clines in their Levy Building office on the Strand. The Strand was the business section of the city near the docks.

"Hello, Charlie," Isaac yelled over the roaring surf. "I know it's right at sunset, but there are so many clouds, I can't see the sun. I'm checking to see if we have a 'brick-dust' sky."

Charlie had learned about weather from his father who was a harbor pilot. Papa C had said, "Moisture in the air at sunset, or in the early morning, can cause the whole sky to take on a reddish color. Therefore, the color is considered a forerunner of rain and bad weather."

Some sailors disagreed; they believed only a reddish sky in the morning predicted bad weather. An old folk warning said: *Red sun in the morning, sailors take warning, but red sun at night, sailor's delight.*

"Doesn't look red to me," Charlie said. Instead, he saw a sky covered with rolling puffy clouds. "I noticed the storm warning flags up this morning. What are you expecting?"

"The Weather Bureau in Washington, D.C. is tracking a hurricane. I've been receiving advisories since Tuesday when it passed over Cuba. This morning about 10:30, the D.C. Bureau notified us they had extended the storm warning to Galveston. The hurricane smashed across Florida and into the Gulf of Mexico."

"A *hurricane* is really coming our way?" Charlie asked.

"It's expected to go ashore east of here. If it does, we'll be on the good side, and we probably won't have too much damage. The telephone at the Bureau has been ringing since the flags went up at 10:35—people wanting information. I told them not to be fooled by today's sunshine. For safety's sake, they would be wise to seek high ground well in advance of the storm. Most likely, we'll get a bad overflow."

"Some people don't pay attention to the warnings," Charlie said.

"You're right," Dr. Cline said. "Most folks take it for granted this storm will behave like the ones they've gone through in the past. Maybe it will, but I'm keeping an eye on it."

When Charlie and Maggie got home, Charlie told his mother about seeing Dr. Cline and what the forecaster had told him. He got the *Galveston Daily News* and looked for the local weather story. He found it on page eight, and he read it aloud.

"Washington, D.C., Sept. 6—For eastern Texas: Partly cloudy Friday with showers and cooler on the coast. Saturday fair; fresh, possibly brisk, northerly winds on the coast.

"Under the forecast, is another article called, 'Tropical Storm Movement,' " Charlie said. He read:

"Tropical storm, now central over southern Florida, moving slowly northward. Wind freshening to thirty or more on Georgia and South Carolina coasts. Center will probably move slowly northward. Wind will begin to increase from northeast along middle Atlantic coast Friday."

"From what Dr. Cline told you, the storm has changed course since the newspaper went to press," Mama said.

"Now, it's headed toward us?" asked Maggie.

"It seems so, but thank goodness they don't expect it to come all the way to Galveston."

After the family ate supper, Charlie washed the dishes, and Maggie dried them. Each night, they took turns washing or drying.

"Let's change our routine," he said to Maggie. "I'll wash every night, and you can dry."

"No, I won't agree to that," she said. "The one who washes gets finished sooner."

"By the way," Charlie said, "I forgive you for forcing me to go *swimming* with you today."

"That's nice of you, Charlie."

"Only because the ball game was called off."

She popped him with the dishtowel. He threw soap-suds at her. They both laughed.

Mama reminded Charlie and Maggie she wanted them to read at least one book before school started. Charlie called to Spatter and went to his bedroom. He had chosen *Huckleberry Finn*. Spatter jumped up on Charlie's bed and looked out the window. He barked.

Charlie wiped sweat off his forehead. He walked over to raise the windows as high as they would go and to see why Spatter barked. As his hands touched the wooden window frame, he glanced at the street below.

In the shadows caused by the street light stood the man. Charlie left the window long enough to turn off the light in his room. Now, he could see better but not be seen. Again, he wondered what the stranger wanted and how long he had stood there.

A quiver went through Charlie's body. He talked quietly to Spatter. "Two problems . . .

"Will the hurricane in the Gulf strike Galveston?

"And is this strange man a danger to my family and me?"

Chapter 3

Rain

$\mathcal{C}$harlie wanted someone else to see the man who watched their house. He left the window and bolted down the hall to Maggie's bedroom.

"Come quick," he said. "The man I told you about is out front again."

Maggie jumped up and rushed to his room. She looked out a window. "I don't see anyone," she said.

"Now, I don't either. He's gone."

"Are you sure you saw someone out there? What was he doing?" Maggie asked.

"Yes, I'm positive I saw him," Charlie told her. "And he's the same person I see all the time. He always lurks in the shadows across the street and stares at our house."

"All right, I believe you," Maggie said. "I'll stay in here for awhile to see if he comes back. Leave the light off."

They sat cross-legged on Charlie's bed. Both watched across the street for the man. Spatter snuggled into Charlie's lap and took a nap. After a few minutes, Maggie said, "School's going to start in about three weeks—on October 1. I'm looking forward to sixth grade."

"I'm not. I'll miss playing baseball in the evenings because of homework, and my summer job will end. Loading boxes on railroad cars is hard work, but it develops muscles, and I like making the money."

"Do you think the strange man will come back tonight?" Maggie asked. "If Papa C were only here! He'd find out what the man is up to. Do you miss Papa C as much as I do?"

"Yes, I'll always miss him. When he disappeared, I couldn't believe he drowned. I expected to see him any time. I don't look for him anymore, though. I know he isn't coming back."

Charlie closed his eyes and pictured his father. He thought Papa C had been handsome with his dark brown hair and nearly black eyes.

"He told me he couldn't stand the feel of the salty spray on a beard when he was working out on a boat," Charlie said aloud. "That's why he never had one—or a mustache either."

"I know he was a good harbor pilot," Maggie said.

Thinking their own thoughts about Papa C, they sat in silence until Mama came to tell them goodnight. "It's time you two went to bed."

"I'm going," Maggie said. But when Mama left the room, Maggie told Charlie, "If the strange man shows up, come get me again."

Charlie lay on his bed and tried to read. When he couldn't keep his mind on the story, he dropped the book on the floor, closed his eyes, and gave in to the thoughts spinning like tops in his brain.

Maggie's right. If Papa C were here, he would get rid of that man.

Finally, he said, "Come on, Spatter. Let's go outside."

Charlie and Spatter walked out the front door close to midnight. Charlie looked up at the sky. The moon shone brightly, unmarred by a stray cloud here and there. A brisk wind provided a cool breeze. "The hurricane must have decided not to come to Galveston," he said to Spatter.

Charlie glanced across the street. "*He* has probably gone for the night, but I have a feeling he will show up again," he muttered. "Spatter, if you're ready, let's go to bed."

Charlie's mother met him at the front door. "I woke up and thought I'd check the weather," she told him.

"The sky is clearer than it was earlier," Charlie said.

"Good! Did Spatter wake you to take him out, or haven't you been to bed?" she asked.

"I didn't feel sleepy. I had too many things on my mind. After supper, when I went to my room, I saw that man watching our house again."

"Maybe he's someone who walks at night and stops to rest. He hasn't done anything to us, so I'm sure there's a reasonable explanation for why you see him. Hurry and get to sleep. It's very late. I'll be waking you before you know it."

"I'm on my way," Charlie told her.

Charlie went to work at the railroad freight depot early in the mornings, Monday through Saturday. As one of the younger workers, he made fourteen cents an hour and got off work earlier than the older boys who received wages of sixteen cents per hour.

After he had worked only two weeks, Charlie coaxed Mama into going to the sporting goods store with him. "I've already saved $5.00 for a down payment on a wheel," he said. "The one I want is the 'Roadster.' It costs $35.00, but I'll be able to pay it off by the end of summer."

Charlie kept his promise. At the end of August, he paid the last installment on the bicycle.

That Saturday, September 8, 1900, Charlie woke up before his mother called him. He walked over to a window and looked out. A rosy pink glow spread across the southern sky.

While the family ate their early breakfast, the sky turned to gray, and raindrops began to fall. "Maybe we *will* have a storm after all," Maggie said.

"I'm going now," Charlie told them as he got up from the table. "Come on, Spatter, let's go to work."

Spatter went everywhere with Charlie. He waited outside the freight depot each day until Charlie finished working.

Mama opened the back door to check the weather. "Take your slicker. The rain has slacked up, but the skies still look threatening. Aren't you leaving a little early, Charlie?"

"I'm not riding my wheel, because I don't want to chance having it sit in the rain all day. I'm going to take a look at the surf, so I'll be doubling back to go to town. I'd better allow myself plenty of time."

"Just don't be late to work," Mama warned.

Low water covered the last four blocks leading to the beach. Charlie waded through the overflow. As he neared the Gulf, he saw enormous waves crash onto shore and send their spray high into the air.

Charlie discussed the scene with other curious onlookers. "Early this morning, Dr. Cline harnessed his horse to a two-wheeled cart and drove up and down the beach," one man said. "He warned residents who live close to the beach—and tourists staying down here—to move to higher ground."

"We live in the upper part of the city," another man said. "We heard about the grand breakers and came to take in the sight."

"Look at that!" Charlie yelled. "The tide's turning over all the bathhouses!"

The small, two-wheeled, brightly painted bathhouses were for rent to bathers who would roll them out into shallow water. After swimming, a bather dressed in the bathhouse and then signaled to the man who rented them. He would use a horse to pull the bathhouse, with the person in it, to shore. This kept sand and water out of the bather's shoes.

In a few minutes, Charlie left the beach to walk the two miles to his work. As he and Spatter crossed Broadway, the street where many grand houses stood, Charlie thought about a trick he and his friends amused themselves with the first of the summer.

He had gotten the idea while looking through Mama's scrap basket for some gray cloth. Mama needed it to patch a hole in his trousers. About the time he found some wadded-up gray felt, Maggie had walked into the room. On a sudden impulse, Charlie slid the felt across the floor. Maggie screamed and jumped up on a chair.

Later, he told Thad and some of the other boys about Maggie's thinking a piece of cloth was a mouse. They wondered if the trick would work on others.

To try out the prank, the boys chose Broadway on a Sunday afternoon. Men and women often strolled there. Charlie tied a black piece of thread to the "mouse" he'd made by sewing and stuffing the gray felt. He placed it on the edge of the sidewalk with the thread leading across the walk into some bushes. The boys hid in the bushes to wait for their prey.

Each time someone walked by, Charlie or Thad pulled the thread, causing the "mouse" to scurry across the sidewalk. Nearly all the ladies screamed, and the men beat at the "varmint" with their canes. Several times, when the victims of the joke heard the boys snickering, Charlie and his friends had to take off running to keep from being thrashed with a cane themselves.

Now, on his way to work at the freight depot, Charlie pondered the fact that objects and events weren't always what they appeared to be. The "mouse" that scared the fine ladies was in reality a piece of harmless gray felt; so could the high tide, that most people considered a forerunner of simply a bad overflow, really be a warning of dangerous weather ahead?

Rain began to fall as Charlie and Spatter neared the Levy Building that housed the Weather Bureau. The rain gave Charlie an excuse to duck inside before walking the other five blocks to the freight depot. He wanted to hear the newest weather report from Dr. Cline.

"Spatter, you sit here. I won't be long," he said. Spatter took his place under the eaves just outside the door.

When Charlie stepped into the office, he saw Dr. Cline talking on the telephone. While Charlie waited, he heard him say to the caller, "At 5:00 this morning, the tide was four and one-half feet above normal, and in spite of a north wind, it continues to rise. If you live within three blocks of the beach, go to higher ground until this is over."

Chapter 4

The Surf

As soon as Dr. Cline hung up the telephone, it rang again, so Charlie knew his friend had no time to chat with him. He waved to the weatherman and left.

At the loading dock, Charlie checked in and reported to the man in charge.

"Morning, Boy. I see you got wet," the boss said.

Charlie nodded. "Good morning. Have you seen the Gulf?" he asked.

"No, I haven't been down there, but I hear it's quite a spectacle," the man said. "We've had high water before. It's a bother, and it'll probably do some damage to lawns and fences. But don't worry. The Gulf will spend itself before long."

Another man working with them told Charlie, "The gutters along most of the streets are already overflowing in the low areas. Of course, Broadway isn't flooded since it runs along the highest ground on the island. Believe me, the water will recede before that happens."

"Oh, I'm not worried," Charlie said. "I'm used to overflows."

About mid-morning, rain fell in such a downpour that Charlie's boss called him aside. "Boy, I think you'd better go on home. From what I hear, there's a strong north wind keeping the Gulf waters back. If that wind shifts, the water may get deep in the streets, and you may not be able to get home."

Charlie and Spatter ran all the way to the Levy Building. Ducking inside to catch his breath, and anxious to learn the latest news on the storm, Charlie headed for the Weather Bureau office. People crowded the halls. He heard a woman say the telephone lines were so busy, she had to come in person to inquire about the weather.

One of the weathermen spoke to the group. "The tropical storm is in the Gulf, south or southeast of Galveston; the barometer is slowly falling. We think the winds will shift to the northeast, east, and probably to the southeast by morning. If you live near the beach or in a low part of the city, move to high ground."

Because of the crowd and all the confusion, Charlie didn't try to talk to Dr. Cline. Anyway, he wanted to take another look at the Gulf.

Charlie hoped the rain would let up before he started out again. He and Spatter stood just inside the entrance to the Levy Building. As he looked out through the partly opened door, Charlie spied a familiar horse and buggy. Mama had stopped the horse to let two women cross the street.

"Look, Spatter, Mama's come to get us." Charlie ran out waving his arms to get his mother's attention.

The wet boy and dog climbed into the buggy.

"Maggie and I came to town and bought groceries," Mama said. "I'd planned to come back later and pick you up when you finished work. I didn't want you to walk in this downpour."

"We went by the freight depot to find out if you might get off early, and a man told us you'd already left," Maggie added.

"I thought we'd catch you walking home," Mama said, "but Maggie insisted we'd find you at the Weather Bureau Office."

"I knew where you'd go," Maggie told him.

"You were right," Charlie said to Maggie. "When my boss told me I could leave for the day, I stopped to see Dr. Cline. I didn't get to talk to him. But I heard another man telling folks the storm is still in the Gulf, and if they live in low places or near the beach to move to higher ground."

"Our home is seven blocks from the Gulf, so I'm sure we'll be fine," Mama said.

"Will you drive us down by the beach?" Charlie asked. "Everyone says the breakers are getting bigger."

"Please, Mama," Maggie begged. "A storm is so exciting!"

"Don't wish for one," Mama said. "Last evening, Mrs. Brewster paid me extra for her dress, and I planned to treat you two to lunch at Murdock's Restaurant today. If the weather gets any worse, though, we'll have to put it off until another time."

"I won't wish for anything to keep us from going to Murdock's," Maggie said and laughed.

"A little rain won't hurt us. We'll have fun," Charlie said. "And since Murdock's is built out over the surf, we can eat and watch the waves at the same time."

"We'll see," Mama said. "First, we'll go down by the Midway and take a look at the surf there. We heard a clerk in the store talking about it. Afterward, we'll let the weather determine whether we go to Murdock's or go home."

"I guess that's fair enough," Maggie said.

The rain slacked up a bit as they neared the beach, but Breeze, the horse, became skittish from the sound of crashing waves and the water it had to walk through. Papa C had named the horse Breeze, because he said it trotted along as smooth as a light summer wind.

When they were two blocks from where the beach should be, they rode through Gulf water. "The waves are rolling far inland," Mama said. "We'd better leave Breeze and the buggy here. We'll have to walk the rest of the way through the water, so you two take off your shoes—they cost $1.50 a pair." She also took off her shoes and stockings, and she held up her long skirt as she stepped down from the buggy.

Charlie tied Breeze to a fence post of a vacant house.

They squeezed together under Mama's umbrella, even though the blowing rain had already wet their clothes. They headed for the Midway.

The Midway consisted of a crowded group of wooden structures covering about ten blocks of the beach. Merchants sold seashells, salt-water taffy, satin pillows, postcards, and other souvenirs to the tourists. Charlie especially liked the games at the penny arcade.

Three large wooden buildings, set on trestles and tall piles, stretched out over the water. One was a three-tiered circular arena used for dancing and moonlight band concerts. The other two buildings contained bathhouses. One, the twin-domed Pagoda Bathhouse, was two blocks long.

Hundreds of curious onlookers already filled the Midway. Streetcars regularly delivered more men and women, many dressed in their finest clothes. Charlie saw women in long silk dresses with fancy beribboned and feathered hats. He saw men wearing three-piece suits and holding straw hats on their heads. Some carried umbrellas which the wind soon turned wrong side out or ripped apart.

A few people with foresight arrived in bathing suits. Pushed along by the wind, those new to the scene scurried through pools of water and spent waves to reach the Midway. Other people, soaked to the skin from rain and the splashing of waves, caught the streetcars back to town.

The atmosphere of excitement seemed contagious. People laughed and elbowed their way in front of others for a better look. But occasionally, someone's temper flared at being jostled from a spot with a good view.

Charlie smelled the familiar odors of boiling clams and steaming frankfurters coming from the food vendor carts. As he, Maggie, and Mama picked their way among the crowd to reach the Midway, the cool water and the squishy sand underneath felt soothing to Charlie's feet.

A gust of wind turned Mama's umbrella inside out. Unable to right it, she pitched it aside. "No matter," she said. "It's useless against this blustery wind."

At last, they reached a place where they could see. Monstrous waves roared and crashed against the pilings that supported the huge bathhouses. The sight left the family speechless for a few minutes. Spatter stayed by Charlie's side until Charlie picked him up and held him close. The dog quietly whined next to Charlie's ear, and he licked the rainwater running down Charlie's face and neck.

Mama, Charlie, and Maggie watched in awe of the pounding breakers. The stairways and platforms leading from the beach to the bathhouses began to give way. As each section fell, the planks were washed and blown along the beach.

The platform supporting a photographic studio at one end of the Pagoda Bathhouse began to sway. One wicked wave after another rose to crash against it. Finally, the studio collapsed and fell into the sea. A loud gasp rose from the crowd. The people instinctively moved back, as if they expected the whole bathhouse to fall. A man collided with Charlie and stepped on his foot. People pressing close behind him kept Charlie from falling down.

"Let's get away from here," Mama called over the thunderous sounds of the surf and other small buildings breaking apart. "We're going home."

Most of the crowd lingered, because they hadn't yet satisfied their curiosity.

To leave the Midway, the family had to weave their way through droves of eager newcomers headed in the opposite direction. Charlie got separated from Mama and Maggie. A woman, pushing her way toward the beach, shoved Charlie into another person.

"Pardon me," Charlie said to the man he had bumped.

The man turned, and Charlie thought his heart would explode. It was the stranger! Charlie recognized the scrawny man with the heavy brown beard and mustache as the one he'd seen watching their house. He quickly glanced around for his mother or sister, but he couldn't see either of them.

The man glared at Charlie with piercing eyes so dark brown they were almost black.

Those eyes, Charlie thought, and he ducked his head to avoid them. "I-I'm sorry," he stammered, as men, women, and children pushed all around them.

The man frowned with a puzzled expression and continued to glare at Charlie.

I must get away, Charlie thought. *There's something scary about this man . . .Why is he looking at me like that?*

"I-I have to go." Charlie choked out the words.

Charlie ran. When he saw he had headed back toward the Midway, he stopped and turned around. He joined some others hurrying away from the angry Gulf. He looked for Spatter, but he didn't see him. He hoped the dog had followed Mama and Maggie.

As he passed near the stranger, Charlie glanced at him. People brushed against the man, but he stood his ground. His eyes followed Charlie.

After forcing his way through the mob of people, Charlie ran as fast as he could in water that reached the calves of his legs. He noticed how much harder he had to struggle to make his way against the wind than he did earlier. He headed for the spot where he had tied Breeze. Mama, Maggie, and Spatter waited for him.

"Mama, I saw him again, and ..." Charlie said breathlessly.

"Never mind who you saw, Charlie," Mama told him. "Get in the buggy. We don't have time to talk. The water has gotten deeper, and the waves are lapping at Breeze's legs. We must get home where we'll be safe!"

"The wind's blowing stronger, too," Maggie said.

Charlie settled into his seat, disappointed with himself. *I'm a coward! I had a chance to ask the man who he was and why he watched our house. And I ran away.*

Charlie didn't mention seeing the stranger again. He tried to put the incident out of his mind.

Chapter 5

Giving Shelter

*W*ater filled the streets. When the family got home, Maggie said, "Our yard is full, too. We'll have to wade to get in the house."

"I'm hungry. Will we eat soon?" Charlie asked.

"I'll prepare it right away," Mama told him. "You put Breeze in his shed, and Maggie, you help me carry the food in the house."

After they ate, Charlie and Maggie spent their time looking out windows to check the progress of the storm. The wind, still blowing from the north, steadily increased. It caused the rain to batter the windows at the back of the house.

When the back door blew open, Mama locked it and shoved the kitchen table against it. "Charlie, get the *News* and let's see what it forecasts for today. I didn't read it this morning," she said.

Looking for the weather report, Charlie sat at the kitchen table and leafed randomly through the newspaper. He wondered if he'd find another article on the debate as to when the twentieth century began. The Pope at the Vatican in Rome had said it would be the nineteenth century until January 1, 1901, and the *Galveston Daily News* had gone along with the Pope. Other people disagreed. They thought the twentieth century began January 1, 1900. Charlie couldn't make up his mind which side he favored.

He stopped to read the cartoons on page ten. When he laughed, Maggie went to look over his shoulder.

"In the background, you can see a man and woman playing tennis. And here are her mother and father sitting on a bench under a tree," Charlie said, pointing.

"I can see, Charlie. You don't have to explain it to me. The father says to the mother, 'Say, Sal, this here new boarder is entirely too fresh. He ain't been here three hours, and I heard him holler *fifteen love* to our Mary.' He didn't understand it was a tennis term."

"Now, who's explaining?" Charlie asked. "The bottom one is my favorite. A man sitting at a table, eating, says to his servant, 'John, have you given the gold fish any fresh water?' The servant answers, 'No, sir; they haven't drunk all they've got.' I really like that one."

"I thought you'd like the one about tennis the best, because it mentions *love,*" Maggie teased.

Charlie slammed the newspaper down on the floor and stood up. "Why would you say that?" he asked her.

"Your face is getting as red as your hair, Charlie. Did I hit on the truth? Do you have a girlfriend?" Maggie backed away from her brother. "Now don't throw a tantrum!"

Mama stepped between them. "Listen to me, you two. I'll have none of your bickering this afternoon! Charlie, pick up the newspaper. Find the weather news like I told you to do while I put away these canned goods."

Reluctantly, Charlie gathered up the strewn papers and found the weather report on page eight. He read:

"For eastern Texas: Rain Saturday, with high northerly winds; Sunday rain, followed by clearing.

"It doesn't sound as if we're going to have a bad storm," he said.

As he started to fold up the newspaper, Charlie noticed an article titled, "Storm on Florida Coast." After scanning it quickly, he told his mother, "This says the tropical hurricane from Jamaica struck the Florida coast Wednesday morning. No damage was done in Miami, but considerable damage has been done in West Palm Beach."

"And now it's in the Gulf," Mama said. "And we don't know *where* it will make landfall next."

In early afternoon, Charlie watched out a front window that faced south toward the Gulf. "It's still raining. Water is over our third step."

Without commenting, Mama threw a blanket over her head and walked out the front door. She hurried across the porch and down to where the water covered three steps. She bent over and stuck one finger in the water. She put the finger to her lips.

Back inside, she threw off the wet blanket and told her children, "I tasted salt. Water is coming from the Gulf, not just from the rain. We are having a bad overflow for the Gulf to come in seven blocks. Surely, it will start to recede soon."

An hour passed with the water still rising. Maggie said, "I hope Breeze is all right. The water must be three feet deep, because it's about a foot from the top of our picket fence."

Apprehension showed on Mama's face for the first time. "Perhaps we'd better consider going uptown. We don't know how deep the water will get before this blows over. I think we should get to higher ground while there's still time."

"Breeze will have a hard go of it, but he can carry us through this if we take it slow and easy," Charlie said.

"Oh, Mama, let's stay here," Maggie pleaded. "I'm having fun watching the water, and the rain will probably stop before long. Can't we stay?"

"It's not the rainwater I'm concerned about," Mama said. "This is the worst overflow I've ever seen. I want to call Aunt Lily and Uncle Elmo to see how they are faring, and then we'll get ready to leave."

She went to the telephone and turned the crank several times, saying, "Central? Can you hear me, Central?"

Mama hung up the receiver. "The telephone is dead. Our line must have blown down," she said. "Get ready to go."

While Mama gathered together rain slickers and quilts and blankets upstairs, the light went off.

"Now, we've lost the electricity, too. You just can't depend on it," Charlie said to Maggie.

"I know. It seems to go off with the least little blow," she said. "It's almost dark in here—what with all the clouds outside."

The Byrds' house had received electricity for only a few months. They continued to keep kerosene lamps handy, because the lights went off frequently.

Someone knocked on the front door. Charlie opened it. Mr. and Mrs. Hill, the next-door neighbors, stood there dripping wet.

"We need shelter," Mr. Hill said. "The water is getting deeper, and the wind has changed to northeast—growing stronger all the time. Our house is not built as sturdy as yours, so we decided to come over here until this is over. That is, if you don't mind."

"We had to paddle through water up to our waists! I felt like a duck." Mrs. Hill giggled.

Charlie liked the Hills, although he thought Mrs. Hill sometimes acted as if she weren't thinking straight. She seemed to always laugh at the wrong things.

One time, when Charlie saw her at the pharmacy, she had said she was after medicine for her husband, who was so sick he couldn't get out of bed. Then she started laughing. In the midst of high-pitched giggles, she proceeded to tell Charlie what a terrible fever Mr. Hill had.

That day, when he got home, Charlie mentioned the incident to his mother. Mama said, "I feel sure the woman doesn't consider her husband's illness funny. I've noticed her laughing when she gets nervous or upset."

"That's an odd way to show you're upset," Charlie remarked.

"Don't fault her. People react differently to stress. I'm sure she can't help it," Mama had said.

When Mama heard the Hills talking in the downstairs parlor, she came down and served them cups of hot coffee. Water had soaked their clothes, and Mrs. Hill's damp yellow hair stuck to the sides of her face.

"Just imagine! Wet ducks sitting in your parlor drinking coffee! Quack, quack," said Mrs. Hill, giggling again.

"She looks like a *drowned* duck," Maggie whispered to Charlie.

"Come with me, and I'll get you dry clothes and find some for Mr. Hill," Mama told the woman. "We were just about to leave for higher ground. I have extra slickers that belonged to my husband. You two can borrow some and come with us—we'll make room in our buggy."

Mrs. Hill changed her clothes upstairs. By the time the women came down carrying a shirt and pants for Mr. Hill, several rain slickers, and a pile of quilts, the water had reached the top of the Byrds' fence.

"It's too late," Mr. Hill said. "The wind gusts are getting stronger by the minute. There's no way we can survive driving a buggy through that kind of wind, along with four-foot-deep rushing water. We've waited too long to leave."

"I'm sure we'll all be safe here," Mama said. "This house is strong, and I'm pleased to have your company. Let's brew fresh coffee. And I need to start cooking some supper for everybody."

Charlie stared out a front window. Suddenly, he cried, "Look! I can see lumber and rooftops in the water. Houses toward the beach are blowing away! Oh! There goes our shed!"

Everyone peered out the windows. "The water is almost as high as our porch," Maggie exclaimed. "What will happen to Breeze? We must save him!"

"I feel terrible about the horse, Maggie," Mama said. "But what can we do?"

Maggie ran away from the window to sit on the sofa. She buried her head in her hands and sobbed.

Suddenly, a bumping sound from the porch startled Charlie. The others heard it too. They all glanced toward the front door.

"What's making that racket? Is someone trying to get in?" Mrs. Hill asked nervously.

Debris cluttering the downtown area.
Photo by H. H. Morris, long-time Galveston photographer

Wreckage in a residential area.

When part of this elementary school collapsed,
the desks remained bolted to the floor.

Residential
area.

Residential
area close to
the beach.
Residents
looking
through the
debris for
their
belongings.

Chapter 6

High Water

Charlie turned the door handle to investigate the noise. A gust of wind full of rain blew the door back hard and knocked him to the floor. Holding onto the heavy wooden door, he pulled himself up. With his hands grasping the door facing, he leaned out so he could get a view of the porch.

"Breeze is here!" he yelled to the others. Struggling against the wind, Charlie made his way out onto the porch. Waves splashed their salty water around his feet. He grabbed a handful of the horse's mane and led him inside the house.

The horse whinnied. Spatter raced around the wide entry hall barking and wagging his nub of a tail, as if he were glad to see a good friend. Maggie ran and threw her arms around Breeze's neck. She wrinkled up her nose. "You don't smell so good wet," she told the horse.

"Hold him while I go to my room to get a rope," Charlie said to Maggie.

Mr. Hill shook his head. Mrs. Hill held her nose and snickered. Mama sighed. "When I asked what we could do, I didn't think of bringing him into the house."

Mrs. Hill giggled in a loud shrill voice. Finally, everyone else laughed with her. They stopped when they heard a pounding on the back door. "I hope that's not another horse who wants in," Mama joked as she started toward the kitchen to unlock the door.

"Wait, Polly," Mr. Hill said. He moved the kitchen table out of the way. "Let me open the door for you. We don't want the wind to wrench it from its hinges." When he turned the doorknob, he put the side of his body and all his weight against the door to keep it from being blown open too violently.

Mama's uncle and aunt, Elmo and Lily Herman, fought the wind to get into the house. Mama hugged them. Besides her children, they were her only living blood relatives.

"I'm so glad you're all right," Mama cried. "I tried to telephone you earlier, but the line was dead. How did you get here?"

"We came in the rowboat I use for fishing," Uncle Elmo answered. "It was hard to keep the boat steady enough to tie it to a post on your porch, but I did it. We climbed out directly onto the porch—no steps to climb this time!"

"We were tossed about so much, we almost didn't make it," Aunt Lily said. "It's dangerous out there. The wind is blowing pieces of wood and slate from roofs through the air so hard they are turned into deadly weapons."

The aunt and uncle lived two blocks farther from the Gulf than the Byrds, but their house was smaller and not as strongly built as their niece's house.

"We wanted to check on you, and anyway, your house is safer than ours," Uncle Elmo said. "But I thought at times we wouldn't get here—the weather seemed to get rougher after we started out."

"Well, you're all right, and that's what matters," Mama told them.

Mama and Mrs. Hill wrapped blankets around the dripping couple to warm them, and Mama said, "I'll go upstairs to get you some dry clothes. You drink this coffee while it's still hot. The gas went off right after I made it, but that was only a few minutes ago."

"Don't be surprised when you see a horse in our entry hall," Maggie told them. "Charlie brought Breeze in to protect him from the elements."

"The poor thing couldn't survive for long out there," Aunt Lily said.

After Uncle Elmo changed into dry clothes, he and Mr. Hill sat together and discussed the storm. Charlie could hear fragments of their conversation. Part of the time, the men spoke in quiet tones, and he couldn't understand them. He thought they both looked funny dressed in Papa C's shirts and pants that were too big for them.

"The wind is now gusting from the northeast," Mr. Hill said in a quivering voice.

"We may be receiving a direct hit. The hurricane was *supposed* to go inland around Mississippi or Louisiana," Uncle Elmo said in almost a whisper. He fingered a loose button on the borrowed shirt he wore.

Mama walked over to the men. "I just looked out the windows. The Gulf water has covered the top of our front and back porches. It's beginning to seep under the doors."

"We were thinking we had best roll up the rug, and take it and your best furniture upstairs," Uncle Elmo told her.

While the men moved the heavier furnishings, Charlie, Maggie, Aunt Lily, and Mrs. Hill took lamps, books, and knickknacks to the second floor.

Mama carried the large family Bible and a cut glass vase Papa C gave her on their last wedding anniversary.

At first, Spatter ran up and down the steps with them. Then he made a beeline to the kitchen and came back carrying his tin food bowl. He took it upstairs and put it down near the other articles from the ground floor. Everyone laughed.

"Spatter, we see you're protecting your favorite possession," Charlie said. "Now, come on and help us with the rest of the moving."

When they finished, Uncle Elmo got the ax from the back porch and said, "Polly, I'll cut some holes in your floor to let in the rising water. It sounds drastic, but if the water keeps getting higher, letting it in may keep the house from floating away."

"And we should also open the windows and doors to ease the pressure from the wind," Mr. Hill added.

The women and children went about raising windows. After the men opened the doors, they chopped holes in the flooring. Water flowed through the doorways and seeped up through the openings in the floor. Washed-in trash soon floated throughout the downstairs.

Wind whistled through the rooms. It whipped the heavy draperies from the windows as if they were dry, brown leaves on a tree in autumn.

"Uncle Elmo!" Charlie called from a front window. "A man is struggling through the water in front of our house."

Uncle Elmo yelled to the man, "You, there—come inside!"

Almost to the point of collapsing, the man labored, half swimming and half walking, to make his way to their door. "I don't think he can manage it alone," Mr. Hill said, so he and Uncle Elmo waded down the flooded front steps to help him into the house.

The man flopped down in about a foot of water on the floor. When he caught his breath, he told them, "I'm trying to get home—I work in the north part of the island. The bay is flooding from the north, and it has met the Gulf. The whole of Galveston is underwater!"

The bay, the body of water north of Galveston, separated the island from the mainland. Only a long wagon bridge and the railroad track connected Galveston Island to the rest of the Texas coast.

Mama handed the man a cup of lukewarm coffee, two biscuits leftover from breakfast, and a quilt. "You're shaking and cold. Wrap up in this and try to get warm."

"You can stay here with us where you'll be safe," Uncle Elmo told him.

"No, I must get to my wife and children," the man said. "As soon as I've rested, I'd best go on. If I don't make it, tell my wife I tried. Here's her name and address on this paper."

After the man left, Maggie said, "He seemed so tired. I hope he gets home."

It wasn't long before Charlie, with his pants' legs rolled up, stood in knee-deep water. He held Spatter in his arms.

Maggie tied the skirt of her dress up in a knot at her left thigh. The wet ruffle at the bottom stuck to her right leg. She twisted a handkerchief in her hands, and every now and then, she wiped her eyes.

"This isn't fun anymore," she said. "Did you ever think you'd see a boat in front of our house? Well, there's a huge fishing boat coming down our street right now!"

"Don't worry," Charlie said. "We'll be all right."

When the water continued to inch up, Mama told everyone, "Come with me. Let's go upstairs. We'll get into dry clothes again and wait this thing out up there."

Charlie looked at Breeze. He thought about why he'd bought the long piece of rope he used to tie the horse. Until he tied Breeze to the banister of the stairway, he'd kept the rope hidden under his bed.

In the middle of the summer, Charlie had told Thad about the man he'd seen watching their house. Thad had gotten all excited and said, "Maybe he wants to rob your house! He could be checking to see if anyone is there. Or, he may be planning to snatch you or Maggie! He may want to take both of you away to be his slaves!"

"What do you think I should do?" Charlie had asked.

"You could tell the police," Thad said. "But until the man actually does something wrong, they won't arrest him. And when he does do something, they may not be able to find him."

"If it won't do any good to tell the police, what else can I do about the man?" Charlie asked.

"I think we should take matters into our own hands," Thad said. "We can set a trap for him."

"What kind of trap?"

"A trap to capture him," Thad said. "You told me he always stands in the same spot. We can take a long rope and tie a slip-knot in it. Then we can lay it out on the ground in a big circle—we'll cover it with grass and leaves so he doesn't see it."

"You're thinking we can hide, wait for the man to show up, and when he does, pull the rope quickly and catch him by the ankles."

"That's the idea!" Thad said. He looked pleased with himself for thinking of the plan.

"But what will we do with him after we catch him?" Charlie asked.

"I haven't figured out that part yet," Thad admitted.

"We could question him," Charlie said. "We could say we wouldn't let him go until he told the truth about what he was doing there."

"But if he refused to tell the truth, we couldn't keep him tied up forever, and he'd know that."

"Maybe, when we get him, if we threaten to take him to the police, he'll go away and watch someone else's house," Charlie said.

"At least we'll scare him," said Thad.

The next Saturday evening, right after supper, Charlie and Thad set their trap. Charlie had bought a long rope at the hardware store. They laid it out in a big circle as planned. After covering it with grass and leaves, the boys hid in some nearby bushes. With the end of the rope in Charlie's hands, ready to be yanked, they waited. At ten o'clock, the man hadn't shown up, and Thad had to go home. But the boys didn't give up.

Charlie hid the rope under his bed, and the following Saturday, they set out again to catch the stranger. About eight o'clock, as they waited in the bushes, they heard footsteps. They peeked out.

"Is that him?" Thad asked.

Charlie nodded yes.

"Get ready," Thad whispered. "When he gets inside the rope's circle, jerk it hard. He'll fall down, and I'll go out and sit on him until you get there. But remember to keep the rope pulled tight around his ankles, so he can't get away."

The boys watched as the man neared the spot where the rope lay hidden. Charlie held the end of the rope firmly in his hands. One more step, and the man would be in the circle. As he took the step, he kicked at the pile of leaves, and his foot caught on the rope. He bent over and felt under the grass and leaves. He lifted up the rope and looked at it. Then he pitched it aside and strolled on down the street.

That night, the man didn't stand and watch, but Charlie saw him glaring at the house as he walked away.

After the plan failed, Thad had said, "He didn't look dangerous to me. My advice, Charlie, is to forget about him."

Because he saw the man off and on the rest of the summer, Charlie hadn't been able to forget.

Now, thinking of the way the man had looked at him that morning at the Midway, Charlie's concern increased. But more important at the moment, wind and water threatened his home and possibly his life.

Chapter 7

The Hurricane

"What should we do with Breeze?" Charlie asked, as the adults started up the steps to the second floor.

With a slight grin, Mama threw her hands into the air. "What else? Bring him with us."

"Let me do it," Maggie said.

She untied the rope, walked up a few steps, and pulled. Breeze didn't move. Maggie tugged harder.

"Getting this horse to go up the stairs isn't easy," she told Charlie. "He won't go!"

"You keep leading, and I'll get behind him and push," Charlie said.

He put both hands on Breeze's rump. The wet horse felt slippery. Charlie had trouble keeping his hands from sliding off as he pushed.

Breeze slowly moved forward until his front feet rested on the fourth step. Then he stopped. Charlie and Maggie urged and tugged until the horse clopped up more steps. Spatter stayed by Charlie's side, and each time Breeze balked at going farther, he yapped at the horse's feet.

At last, when they reached the upstairs hall at the top of the stairway, Maggie said, "I won't be so quick to offer to lead him downstairs. On second thought, I guess you got the worst *end* of the deal!"

Charlie laughed. "I surely did. We'll switch *ends* when we take him back down."

After tethering Breeze to a doorknob, Charlie and Maggie went into the upstairs sitting room on the front of the house facing south. They joined the others who stood at a few closed windows to watch the storm.

Before long, Mrs. Hill shrieked, "Homes all around us are breaking up and washing away."

"The boards from the downed houses are slamming into other houses and tearing them apart," Uncle Elmo said.

Often, someone ventured into another room to get a different view of the destruction. When Mr. Hill went to take a look, he came back into the sitting room wearing a sad expression on his face.

He put his arms around his wife and told her, "I was standing at a side window in Maggie's bedroom, and I saw our home go down. It leaned over against the Byrds' house and fell apart."

Mrs. Hill buried her face in her husband's chest and cried softly.

Mr. Hill said to Mama, "I'm sorry Polly. Our house took your side porch with it."

Maggie looked out an east window in Charlie's room and screamed. She ran to her mother and threw her arms around her. "I saw two dead people floating by," she cried. "There was a man and a woman. They had their eyes open, but I could tell they were dead!"

"Maggie," Mama said, "this is a tragic thing that's happening. Many people may be killed. Stay here with me."

They watched as the wind ripped shutters off their house. They felt the vibration as the rushing water caused the front porch and the upstairs gallery to collapse.

Later, after checking the storm from every direction, Uncle Elmo reported, "The back porch is gone, too. The wind must be close to a hundred miles an hour. It's blowing from the east, and the panes are shattering on that side of the house. We'd better stay away from all the windows."

Mama put an arm around each of her children and said, "Come, let's go sit together." She guided them to a corner opposite the windows. They sat on the floor, the mother in the middle. Spatter climbed into Charlie's lap and whined.

Mr. and Mrs. Hill huddled together on the high-backed settee. Uncle Elmo and Aunt Lily pulled two chairs across the room to sit side by side. It was as if all of them wanted to be near the ones they loved the most. If the house went down, they would go together. From time to time, one or all of the small groups could be seen praying.

Maggie checked on Breeze in the hall. She informed the others, "The water's almost to the top of the stairs."

Soon, the sloshing of water, along with the bumping of furniture against the downstairs ceiling, joined the outside sounds of wailing wind and objects battering the house.

Charlie had a hard time sitting still. He stood up to stretch and steal a glance out a window. He saw boxes and barrels, parts of wrecked houses, wooden cisterns, chairs, tables, and other furnishings traveling westward in the current over their street.

Another time Charlie looked outside and said, "Here comes a rowboat full of people! They're heading north. I hope they aren't capsized."

"Let me tell them they can climb through a window and take shelter here," Mama said. With salt water spraying their faces, she and Charlie called to the people.

At last, Mama gave up and said, "They weren't far from the house, but they couldn't hear us." She and Charlie sat back down on the floor with Maggie. When water began to cover the floor, they got up and crowded together on a loveseat.

The house creaked and groaned. "It sounds as if it's in pain," Mama said, trying to ease the tension in the room.

"Those noises aren't anything to joke about," Uncle Elmo said. "They mean the timbers supporting the house are beginning to loosen. And there is no indication the storm will end any time soon."

Without warning, the wind blew in the south windowpanes, scattering glass over the room. "Get into the hall, and protect your heads," Uncle Elmo hollered.

Charlie sat on the hall floor with his arms shielding his head and face. His legs formed a shelter for Spatter. He heard other windows shatter. A cold wind moaned through the house like the wail of a night train traveling through a long dark tunnel.

A loud crash caused everyone to uncover their eyes and look up at the ceiling. Blowing water hit them in the face. A section of streetcar rail had been driven through the roof, splitting it apart. The rail had come to rest on the hall floor not far from Breeze. The horse whinnied and pulled at his restraint.

Charlie felt the house move. It swayed back and forth.

"The strong wind and rushing water—and all the debris being driven against the house—is too much for it," Mama cried sadly. "It can't stand up much longer."

Uncle Elmo went to look out a window in Charlie's bedroom. He came back and untied Breeze.

"Why are you letting the horse loose?" Aunt Lily called out.

"Because we're leaving," Uncle Elmo yelled above the storm's din. "We'll be better off taking our chances out there in the water than staying and going down with the house. Go back to the sitting room where some of the windows face west."

"What are we going to do?" Aunt Lily cried.

"The wind has shifted to the southeast. If we go into the water on the west side of the house, the wind and current should take us away from the house, instead of bashing us into it," he explained.

Putting his hands on their shoulders, he prodded them, one at a time, to leave the hall. Once they got back into the sitting room, he said forcefully and without hesitation, "Mr. Hill and I will go first. We will try to help the rest of you when you jump. Do not tarry!"

Silently, the women nodded agreement.

Without further words, Uncle Elmo climbed upon a windowsill and leaped into the raging water. Mr. Hill wavered for an instant, and then he, too, jumped.

"Children, you are next," Mama shouted. "When

you hit the water, grab hold of anything that will float, and hang on."

Maggie clung to her mother until Mama pried her loose and shoved her out the window. Then Charlie saw Mama turn toward him. It was his turn.

Charlie clutched Spatter in his arms. He thought, *I can't do it! My legs won't move. Lord, please don't make me jump into that water.*

The touch of his mother's strong arms urged him, and before he knew it, he tumbled through the window. With his eyes tightly closed, he held his breath and waited for the splash he'd hear when he made contact with the water—before he went under.

He didn't have long to wait, because the surface of the water almost reached the second-story windows.

Ker-plunk! Charlie landed on his stomach. He hit something hard. He felt it move. He opened his eyes. He raised his head a little and looked around. Charlie thought his prayer had been answered. He'd fallen on a piece of someone's roof that floated by at the right time.

He looked for Spatter. He remembered squeezing the dog firmly in his arms as he jumped. A sputtering bark got Charlie's attention. He saw Spatter scrambling in the water to get on the traveling roof. Charlie reached over and pulled the dog up by the skin of his neck. He tucked him under one side of his own body. "You might get mashed, but you won't blow away unless I go too," he told Spatter.

Looking behind him, Charlie saw his uncle hanging onto a back corner of their house. A small porch, turned upside-down, floated close to the house. Uncle Elmo got on it. It still had three upright wooden posts attached. With others, the timbers had once supported the porch from the ground.

Uncle Elmo lay on his stomach and wrapped an arm around one of the heavy support timbers. Mama struggled in the water. Uncle Elmo kept reaching out to her with his free hand. At last he succeeded in helping her climb up beside him.

Near them, Maggie held onto a floating railroad tie and kicked her feet in the water. Charlie knew she attempted to propel herself closer to the upside-down porch and her mother.

Charlie heard a loud roar. At first, he thought it was thunder, but he hadn't seen a lightning flash. He looked back toward his home in time to see large chunks of the roof lift off. On the wind, they sailed over Charlie's head to land somewhere beyond him. The home's second floor, urged by the storm's mighty force, crumbled into a heap. Cherished pieces of furniture—favorite clothing— walls that only moments before had protected human life—took their place in the water, bound for an unknown destination. Charlie turned away.

To the right of Charlie's roof, Mrs. Hill and Aunt Lily rode together on what looked like part of the side of a house. They held hands and clutched at each other's clothes. Charlie thought he could hear Mrs. Hill giggling hysterically.

Then he saw a brutal wave force up a large piece of timber. It struck the two women and knocked them into the current. They groped for something to keep them afloat, but water and debris swept over them. Charlie couldn't see them anymore. Tears mixed with salt water on his face.

Charlie never saw Mr. Hill. He wondered what had happened to him.

Whipped by the wind against Charlie's body, rain and salt water pelted him like bullets. He shivered from the cold, but he kept a firm grip on the roof. It moved freely with the current until it piled up against what was left of a house and wedged there among other rubbish. Water swirled around it.

Charlie looked for the porch holding his mother and Uncle Elmo. It sailed swiftly toward him. He saw Maggie. "I'm glad she's with them," he said to himself.

Angry waves shot way up into the air, and Uncle Elmo's porch rose and fell with them. Before the porch got even with him, Charlie heard a cracking sound and felt his roof move underneath him. Piece by piece, it began to break up. When only a small portion of the roof remained for Charlie to cling to, the porch floated beside him. Charlie jumped. He grabbed hold of one of the support timbers with his right hand. He clasped Spatter tightly under his left arm.

"We made it," he yelled.

His mother reached out and touched his leg. Maggie gave him a weak smile. With his arm, Uncle Elmo batted away a piece of flying slate. No one tried to talk.

The family rode the wildly bobbing porch for hours. When Charlie heard people crying or talking, he supposed they drifted nearby on pieces of wreckage. He saw an uprooted telegraph pole strike a man in the back of the head and knock him into the current. More than once, he saw forms struggling in the water, grabbing at anything washing by. And he heard shrieks as some of them went under.

Charlie wished he could cover his ears and close his eyes, but he had to hold on and watch out for objects hurled by the wind.

As the porch moved through the water, Charlie heard the piercing scream of a woman. This was followed by a crash. He saw a house turn over and disintegrate.

The wind and the flood drove the fragments of the home alongside them. Charlie saw a small wooden cradle caught up in the midst of the wreckage about eight feet away. He heard a baby crying.

Chapter 8

The Baby

*C*harlie turned his head. He didn't want to see the baby drown. He looked at his family. Uncle Elmo, crouched at one corner, gripped a support timber and peered intently in the direction they drifted. Mama and Maggie both lay flat on their stomachs. Each clutched an upright timber with one hand and shielded her head from flying objects with the other. Charlie's folks gave no indication they noticed the wee bed or heard the baby's cry.

There's nothing I can do, Charlie thought.

But he couldn't resist glancing back at the little bed. As he watched, it moved closer until it floated about six feet away. Charlie heard the baby cry again. He realized he would hear that cry the rest of his life if he didn't do all he could to save the child. He retrieved a long narrow board from the water. Repeatedly, he held it out, trying to snag a part of the cradle to bring it to him. He knew if he wasn't careful, he could tip the cradle over.

When he couldn't keep the board steady because of the up and down motion of the water, Charlie gave up. He pitched the wood back into the current.

"In a few minutes, it's going to be dark. If I'm ever going to do it, now is the time," he mumbled. "Spatter, you're on your own." He let go of his dog.

Over the side of the porch Charlie plunged! He started swimming. Even in the turbulent water, how well he could swim surprised him. If debris didn't force him under, he might make it.

He dodged pieces of flying wood and pushed aside a small table. He could see the baby's bed had almost drifted free of other wreckage. He didn't know if it would float by itself.

Charlie swam harder. Just as he reached out to grab the cradle, something struck him on the left side of his head. He inhaled some of the salt water. He choked on it and began to cough. His head throbbed. He put both arms over the block of wood he hadn't seen until it hit him. He held on and tried to keep his head above water. To fight against losing consciousness, he tried to concentrate on the helpless baby.

Before long, he regained his wits. Charlie felt the blackness of night closing in on him. Fear of being carried off by the current, alone in the dark, filled his thoughts, as he looked for the cradle.

Although his eyes seemed to adjust to the darkness, he couldn't see the cradle. He figured the flow of the water had carried it ahead of him. Or, it went under while he recovered from the bash on his head. The porch with his family on it was nowhere in sight either.

Charlie struggled with the rushing flood. He swam with the current moving to the northwest; it was easier than fighting his way across it. Seaweed washed over him, and some clung fast, making swimming even more difficult. Pieces of wood and glass from demolished homes crowded the water. They scraped and cut his body. The salt in the water caused the scratches and cuts to sting, and it burned his eyes. The fishy smell of the sea filled his nostrils.

He squinted, trying to see in the distance. He hadn't gone far when the bobbing cradle appeared right before him. He managed to get a hand on it. At the same time, he caught hold of a drifting railroad tie to keep himself afloat. He noticed a wide strip of cloth tied over the top of the cradle and into a knot on one side. He thought the mother must have placed it there to keep her child from falling out.

With a watchful eye for something sturdy to climb up on, Charlie clung to the railroad tie and the bed. He was glad the baby kept crying, for as long as he heard its wail, he knew it was alive.

Charlie bumped against something, and the water swept the railroad tie away from him. He still clutched the cradle. He had drifted into a tree and could tell it was a large salt cedar. He thought since it hadn't washed away by now, it might withstand the flood.

Charlie grabbed at one of the limbs. He got it, but the force of the water pulled at the bed. He had to get the baby out before the swift current jerked the cradle from his hand. But how? He couldn't turn loose of the limb or the cradle to lift up the baby.

Charlie strained to hang onto the cradle. His hand hurt. He knew he couldn't hold on much longer. Maybe he could use his legs to help. There! One leg touched a limb under the water. He maneuvered his legs toward the unseen limb until he could wrap them around it to anchor himself. He took his hand off the limb to reach for the infant.

He leaned toward the cradle. He pulled at the knot in the wet material stretched over the baby. He couldn't untie it. He tried to slide the fabric out of the way, but the mother had tied it so tightly, he could only move it a little bit at a time. With water splashing against him and the cradle, Charlie kept inching the cloth. When it covered just the baby's legs, he picked up the child by one arm and shoulder and brought it to him. He turned loose of the cradle.

The baby cried louder.

"I probably hurt you," Charlie said. "But it was the best I could do under the circumstances."

Charlie clutched the tiny wet infant to his chest. Using his legs and one hand, he made his way along the underwater limb until he came to where it joined the trunk. Slowly, he worked his way upward to sit on a higher limb. He turned his back to the wind-driven rain and splashing water. He wrapped his legs as tightly as possible around the tree trunk.

The hurricane force wind blew from the south. It tore off Charlie's shirt, pants, and even his underwear. He had lost his shoes and socks in the water, and debris had shredded his clothes. The baby wore only a gown, so Charlie hugged the child closer to his chest to shield it. "I'll keep you as warm as I can," he said.

After awhile, the baby quieted and fell asleep.

Charlie's body tingled with weakness. He shook from the cold, and his teeth chattered. His scratched and bleeding hands ached. His head still throbbed from the blow it had received. Charlie knew it would be easier to turn loose of the tree and let the storm win. But the safety of the baby he held between his body and the tree trunk depended on him.

Charlie thought the wind sounded like a giant wolf howling in the night. It seemed to launch surprise attacks—great gusts against his back—as if it intended to injure the child by forcing Charlie's body into the tree trunk.

Charlie fought the blows to his back. He pushed against each gust so hard, he would nearly fall backward when it let go of him.

"You're not getting us," he yelled at the unseen enemy. The tree swayed and bent. Charlie hung on like the man he once saw breaking a wild stallion.

Occasionally, he heard people's voices. He couldn't see them in the dark, but he assumed they were in other nearby trees. A few times, when lightning flashed, he did see people. A bathtub holding two women floated past him, and he saw someone on a roof. A part of the roof slowly capsized, dragging the person underneath the water.

Charlie estimated he had stayed in the tree about three hours when the wind started to let up, and the lightning stopped. Now that he wasn't compelled to fight a strong wind, he again became aware of the dark. Thinking of the many hours of night left before daylight sent a frightened shiver through his body.

Awhile later, the moon peeked out, and Charlie saw that the water rushed from the opposite direction. He could faintly see a tree limb below him. He shouted, "The water's flowing back to the sea. It's going down!"

Dark clouds still moved across the sky, but now, through open patches, the moon and stars shone brightly. Charlie smiled. For the first time, he felt sure he and the baby would see tomorrow.

Charlie woke with a start. When he realized he had dozed off, his reflexes caused him to clutch the sleeping baby tighter. "I still have you," he said with a sigh and relief in his voice. "Why did I let myself go to sleep? I might have dropped you, or we both could have fallen into the water."

He shook his head to clear it. Charlie saw the first light of dawn, a deep orange glow in the east, surrounded by dark gray puffy clouds. As he watched, the glow changed to a lighter orange, the clouds disappeared, and the sky turned from dark blue to light blue. A giant orange ball peeked over the horizon. As it moved higher in the sky, the sun grew so bright, Charlie couldn't look at it.

He gazed around him. He saw no other people. He sat on a limb about fifteen feet off the ground. Once the floodwater started going down, it had run off quickly. Only scattered puddles remained. Charlie had never been so thankful for a beautiful Sunday morning!

He started to climb down the tree. Holding onto the baby made it difficult. The jostling woke the child. It started to cry again.

Charlie put his left foot on a limb below him. As he started to move his right leg down, he felt something move under his left foot. He thought he had broken the limb. He jerked his left leg back up. He looked below him.

"Copperheads!" he yelled.

Two snakes, each roughly eighteen inches long, lay stretched along the limb. Charlie had stepped on one of them. He didn't know much about snakes, but he could recognize copperheads. And he knew they were poisonous!

Chapter 9

Snakes

*C*harlie's legs could reach only one limb below him, the one where the snakes rested. To get down from the tree, he must step on that limb. He figured he had two choices. He could wait awhile and hope the snakes left. Or, he could try to scare them out of the tree.

"I'm anxious to go look for my family. I don't want to stay here any longer," he said aloud.

Charlie put the baby up on his shoulder and leaned forward, pressing the child gently against the trunk of the tree. With his left arm under the baby's bottom to support it, he gripped a limb with his left hand. With his right hand, he broke off a branch. He hoped it would reach down to where the snakes lay sunning themselves.

He furiously swished the branch below him. When he moved it from his line of vision to find out if the snakes had gone, he saw them moving. But they started *up* the tree *toward* him instead of going *down*! Charlie took a deep breath and told himself to stay calm. Anyone who had survived a hurricane while hanging onto a tree could surely handle a couple of snakes.

One snake inched up the trunk to within two feet of the limb Charlie sat on. Charlie hit at the snake and missed. He almost lost his balance, but he had to try again. Securing the baby as best he could, he swiped hard at the copperhead. He hit his target, but the blow didn't seem to disturb the snake. It didn't budge from the tree trunk. Charlie tried once more. This time, he poked at it until the intruder turned and slithered down the tree.

Charlie looked for the other snake to chase it away. He couldn't see it. He waited a few minutes. He searched all around him. He never found the missing snake, so he cautiously began to make his way to the ground.

The baby continued to cry as Charlie climbed down the tree. Hoping to soothe the child, Charlie talked to it. "Hush, little one," he said. "We're going to be all right. I know you're hungry, and I am too. And I need some clothes. I'm sure there are plenty of houses still standing. We'll find someone to help us and give us food.

"I hope my family made it safely through the storm. I'll put any thoughts that they didn't out of my mind. I'll find them. I know I will. But where? I'll have to look for them. First, I'll get rid of you. I've done my part. But before I leave you, I would like to know if you're a boy or girl.

"I have no idea where I am. But I'm sure the tide moved me northwest from my home—west of town. If I walk toward the sun, I should find the city. I'll get my bearing when I see a familiar landmark.

"There, there, that's better," Charlie said to the child. "You like for me to talk to you, don't you? I'll find some-one along the way to take you, or I'll carry you to the police station. Chief Ketchum will know what to do."

Charlie avoided the pools of trapped water. Where the water had run off, a bad-smelling gray slime, mixed with seaweed, covered the ground. Charlie wrinkled his nose and tried to take shallow breaths. As he put one foot after the other in the muck, it oozed between his toes. It felt thick and slippery. Blood from cuts on his feet left red streaks in his footprints.

He looked around for something to cover his body until he got some clothes. After finding nothing better, he picked up a board about a foot-and-a-half square and held it in front of him. His backside would just have to show!

The farther Charlie walked, the more uneasy he became. Everywhere he looked, he saw destruction. Dead horses, cows, chickens, and dogs and cats lay in the midst of piles of wreckage.

"I hope Spatter didn't get killed," he said.

He saw the bodies of a woman and a young girl. Charlie quickly looked away. He wasn't prepared for that. He got sick at his stomach and had to stop and throw up. As he walked on, he saw more dead men, women, and children.

"I won't think about what could have happened to Mama and Maggie and the others. They have to be all right," he said.

The few upright homes Charlie passed stood in ruin. The hurricane had blown off roofs and caved in parts of houses. It scattered bedding, furniture, cooking utensils, clothing, and window frames. Uprooted trees littered the ground. Some had been driven through homes.

As Charlie wondered if he and the baby were the only human survivors of this devastation, he saw a woman standing in the doorway of a badly wrecked home.

He started toward the woman. "I'll ask if she'll take care of you and give me something to wear," he said to the baby.

With a blank look on her face, the woman stood motionless and stared into space. The only signs of life she displayed were the tears running down her cheeks. The baby cried loudly. The woman didn't appear to notice. Charlie turned away and walked on.

Soon, he passed other men and women. Most wore tattered clothing, and they all looked sad and hopeless.

Blood painted stripes down many faces. Some people had wrapped pieces of fabric around their heads, arms, or legs to bandage wounds.

Charlie heard the quiver of the women's voices and saw their trembling lips. They didn't seem to care that he had a mere piece of wood to hide his nakedness. He asked a man, "Am I going the right way to get to town?" The man nodded yes and pointed.

Charlie came upon several small children wandering about, alone and crying. Like him, a few had no clothes. Were they lost or orphaned? "I wish I could stop to help you," he told the children. "Some grown-ups will come along soon to take care of you." It was all Charlie could do to care for the small infant he carried.

Exhaustion almost overcame him. The gray slime covering the ground made walking difficult. The foul odor caused Charlie to feel sick at his stomach again. He sat down on a mass of trash and cried with the baby.

"This won't accomplish anything, will it?" he said at last to the bundle in his arms. He hadn't realized the child had quit crying until he spoke to it. It looked up at him and smiled. The affection he felt for the baby at that moment embarrassed him.

"I still don't know if you're a boy or a girl," he told the baby. "Of course, I could find out." The thought made Charlie smile. He looked around to see if anyone was watching him. No one was.

Charlie discovered he had rescued a little boy. Having cried out his despair, he cuddled the child in one arm. With renewed hope, he again started toward town. Eventually, he came to a house that had suffered less damage than the others he had seen. It stood upon the usual high pilings. The storm had blown away a section of the roof and broken the windows, but the walls appeared intact. The front door hung askew on its hinges.

Thinking the owners might be at home and have some food, water, and clothes to spare, Charlie made his way up wide, storm-damaged steps to the entrance. "Is anyone home?" he called.

He got no answer.

"I need help. Isn't anyone here?" he yelled louder. He knocked hard on the door.

He heard a noise inside the house.

"I'm a young boy, and I have a hungry baby with me. Please come to the door," he begged.

He heard the bumping sound again.

Charlie felt his face flush. He wanted to yell out that a terrible person must live there, but he took a deep breath instead. He gave the one inside another chance. He called in his loudest voice, "My mother taught me not to walk into someone's home unless they asked me, so please answer. I'm desperate."

Scra-a-pe! The noise sounded like furniture being moved.

Charlie couldn't understand a person's ignoring an appeal for help, but this one refused to see what he needed. If he hadn't heard noises to indicate the house was occupied, he would have gone on in. After all he'd been through, he wouldn't feel bad about taking food from an empty house for the baby and him to eat.

There was a bump and a scrape. *Moo-o-o-o!*

"Who's there? Is that a *cow?*"

Moo-o-o! Moo-o-o!

Charlie struggled to push open the door enough to squeeze through it. Cautiously, he walked into the entry hall. He leaned around the door facing of the room on the right and peeked in. He saw the parlor in complete disarray. Water, along with glass from broken windows, covered the floor. Furniture had floated into a pile against one wall. Much of it ended up overturned or bashed into pieces.

Suddenly, Charlie felt a hard blow on his backside! He fell forward to his knees. Still holding the baby, he looked behind him.

Moo-o-o! Moo-o-o! The cow had slipped up in back of him and poked him with its head.

Charlie got to his feet and rubbed his bottom. "I'm glad you don't have horns!" he said. "But, Bossy, if you're looking for someone to milk you, don't look at me. I've never milked a cow in my life!"

He pushed past the cow and went to the back of the house to find the kitchen. He spied a pan of biscuits on top of the stove. Upon closer inspection, he saw that water filled the pan and soaked the flat cakes of bread. He turned on the faucet over the sink. Nothing came out.

"No water," he said.

As he looked around for other food, the baby began to whimper. Charlie patted him. The child turned his head when Charlie's hand touched his face. With his mouth, he grabbed hold of one of Charlie's fingers and began to suck on it.

"My finger won't fill your stomach, but maybe it will keep you quiet while I look for something to feed you," Charlie said.

He walked through the standing water in the kitchen, searching for any food that hadn't been ruined. On the floor, he saw a heavy black pot filled with a murky liquid. He opened the door to the gas oven. Muddy water trickled out, but he found a slab of cooked beef ribs.

"I'm going to put you down for a few minutes so I can tear off a piece of this meat," Charlie said.

He laid the child in the sink, the driest place in the kitchen. When Charlie pulled his finger out of his mouth, the baby screamed. "One would think I'd be used to your crying by now," Charlie said, "but I wish you'd hush. I'm doing the best I can."

To Charlie, the meat looked delicious, despite the fact it had soaked in floodwater. He held it up to his nose. It didn't smell spoiled. He ripped off a piece and shoved it into his mouth. It had very little flavor, mostly a salty taste. It felt gritty on his tongue. But it was food!

"Before I eat anymore, I'll feed you some so you will stop crying," Charlie told the baby. "I hope it doesn't make you sick, but I can't let you starve."

Charlie put a small piece to the child's mouth. Suddenly, he jerked the meat back. "You don't have any teeth!" he said. "I didn't feel any when you sucked on my finger. I suppose you only drink milk. Where am I going to find a bottle of milk?"

Chapter 10

Aftermath of the Storm

For a brief time, Charlie wondered where he might find some milk. All at once, he slapped his forehead with the palm of his hand and said, "I'm not thinking! The cow! I hope it hasn't wandered off." Charlie left the baby and dashed to the front of the house. He found the cow standing in the parlor.

"I've *seen* people milk cows like you," he said. "It didn't look too hard. One pulls on those spouts, and milk comes out. All I need is a container for the milk to fall into. I remember seeing a black pot on the kitchen floor. I'll get it."

In the sink, the baby kicked his legs, waved his arms, and squalled.

"In a minute I'll have some milk for you to drink," Charlie told the child. "I have no way of washing this pot—probably had beans cooked in it before it got filled with flood water." He swished the liquid in the pot around and poured it out on the floor.

Charlie couldn't find anything to sit on, so he got down on his knees next to the cow. He put the black pot under the animal to catch the milk. The cow moved a few feet away. Charlie scooted close again, and positioned the pot. The cow swished its tail, hitting Charlie in the face, and moved again.

Charlie got up and looked for something he could use to restrain the cow. He found a woman's wet skirt in the water on the floor. He ripped it into strips and tied the strips together to form a makeshift rope. He fastened the cow to a sturdy table.

Again, Charlie went down on his knees and placed the black pot in the right spot under the cow. With his hands, he gently pulled on the cow where the milk was supposed to come out. A few minutes passed, but no milk. He yelled to the crying baby, "I haven't gotten it turned on yet, but I'll get the hang of it soon."

As Charlie worked to force some milk from the cow, he tried to recall how he'd seen other people do it. At last, he hit on the right motion with his hands, and milk spurted into the pot. Charlie grinned at his success. When he thought he had enough, he carried the milk to the kitchen.

He propped the baby up at an angle and tilted the pot of milk to his lips. The child sputtered and almost strangled. Charlie learned in a hurry that an infant could drink only a small amount at a time. "Now, we have another problem to solve," he said. "If only I had a baby bottle! This pot's too big for you to drink out of."

He glanced around the kitchen for something smaller. He saw a tablespoon wedged under an overturned pie safe.

After a half-hour of Charlie's spooning milk into the baby's mouth, the baby closed his eyes and went to sleep lying in the sink.

Charlie ate barely enough of the beef to satisfy the growling in his stomach. Next, he thought he'd better find himself something to wear. He made his way up the rickety steps to the second floor to borrow some clothes. He couldn't go to town in his "birthday suit."

Upstairs, Charlie found clothing the wind had cast about the bedrooms. As he searched through it, picking up one wet garment and then another, he grumbled to himself. The family who lived there must consist of only girls. He couldn't find anything that belonged to a man or boy. But Charlie was in no position to be particular. He found a pink shirtwaist dress about his size. He put it on and buttoned up the front. Its dampness caused the skirt to hug his legs.

When he came back downstairs and picked up the baby, a loud burp startled Charlie. He smiled and said, "I guess that means you enjoyed your meal."

Charlie pulled at the collar of the dress. The lace tickled his neck. As he settled the infant in his left arm, he made a face and turned up his nose in disgust. "I'm tired of your soggy wet diaper!" he said. "But I don't have anything dry to put on you. I could take it off and leave you bare. But that might be a bad idea. I know one thing—I don't like the 'diaper' part of caring for you."

Before leaving the house, Charlie untied the cow. "Thank you for the milk," he said.

Although he expected to find someone who would take the child and look for his mother, he carried along the spoon and the black pot with the remainder of the milk in it.

As he walked in the direction of town, dressed in the frilly pink frock and carrying the baby in his arms, his thoughts turned to his sister. "Wouldn't Maggie laugh if she could see me now?"

When Charlie thought about Maggie, he had a strong feeling she was also thinking of him. And if she were alive, probably Mama, too, had lived through the storm—and Uncle Elmo. Charlie didn't feel as confident about the survival of Aunt Lily and the Hills.

He talked to the baby. "It seems like such a long time since my family and I all rode together on the upside-down porch, and I wondered if any of us would survive. I remember looking from one to the other to see if they heard your cry. That was right before I dove over the side into the rushing current. I guess I conquered my fear of water. I feel real good inside about saving your life, little fellow."

To make his way east on the storm-ravaged island, Charlie veered around piles of broken stone, bricks, and wood that had once made up homes. The trash littering the ground added more scratches and cuts to his already sore feet. Finally, he began to recognize parts of houses that hadn't blown away.

He approached Broadway Avenue on the highest part of the island. He saw that many of the large, strongly built homes, although heavily damaged, still stood. Most streetcar tracks had either disappeared or had been ripped up and twisted. Charlie saw a telegraph pole driven under one track. The same gray mud and seaweed covered the ground and gave off a terrible stench.

Upon reaching the town, he saw destroyed buildings and others with various degrees of damage. The floodwater had washed up the streets' wooden paving blocks. In places, metal from roofs lay rolled up like newspapers.

Men stood in groups, talking in quiet tones. Women, with concern showing on their faces, consoled one another and wept together.

Charlie heard people ask each other how their families fared. From their answers, it seemed nearly everybody had lost loved ones or had family members missing. The few fortunate families who escaped without loss of lives would answer something like, "We're homeless, but we're thankful we're alive," or, "My family survived, and that's all that matters." He heard no one complain about property damage.

Charlie searched the streets for his family. When he met folks he knew, he'd ask, "Have you seen my mother or sister or Uncle Elmo?"

Some answered, "No. I'm sorry," or, "No, but if I see them, I'll say you're alive and looking for them." Many people ignored his question or gave him a quick, "No!" and rushed off to hunt for their own relatives.

As Charlie wandered through the town, he kept an eye out for any woman stable enough to care for the baby. He walked up to one lady to ask if she'd take the child, but he couldn't force himself to say the words.

Instead, he said, "I'm caring for this baby. Do you know where I can get a dry cloth to change his diaper?" Charlie saw no reason to explain why he wore a girl's dress or where he got the baby.

"My clothes have dried," the woman said. "Here, I'll give you a piece of my petticoat—it's hanging in shreds anyway."

Charlie thanked her and sat down on a board to change the diaper. "*She* probably would have taken you. I don't know why I didn't ask her."

He laid the baby on his own legs to keep him out of the stinking mud. It wasn't easy to balance a squirming infant and to keep from sticking him as he unfastened the large safety pin. Charlie pitched the wet diaper to the side. He wrapped the long piece of the lady's petticoat around the baby boy's middle and between his legs several times. When he came to the end of the cloth, Charlie pinned it to the wad of material.

Finished and ready to go on, Charlie noticed something fastened to the inside of the wet diaper he'd thrown aside. He reached over and unpinned it. It was a tightly wrapped piece of oilcloth. In the oilcloth, Charlie found a folded paper. He opened it and read what appeared to be a hastily scribbled note written in pencil. It said:

> House falling apart. If I don't survive take baby.
> Husband dead—no relatives—Name is Joshua
> Elizabeth Packard (mother)

"Well, Joshua, now that I know your name, and your mother's, we'll go to the police station and inquire about her," Charlie said. "And we'll see what we can find out about my family, too."

As Charlie neared the police station building, he saw its roof had caved in and the walls had collapsed in the street. He waited for two men standing nearby to finish their conversation, so he could ask them where he should turn for help.

He heard one man say, "The railroad bridges and the wagon bridge to the mainland are heavily damaged or washed away, and all the telegraph and telephone lines are down. Galveston is cut off from the rest of the world."

"And the city has no electricity, gas or water," the other man said.

"Mayor Walter Jones has called a council meeting for ten o'clock to appoint a relief committee and assign them jobs," the first man said. "There's plenty to do—cleaning up the city, caring for the injured and homeless, distributing food to the hungry..."

"And they'll have to prevent looting and bury the dead," the second man added.

When the men stopped talking and stood shaking their heads, Charlie asked, "Is there anyone who can help me find my family?"

"Not yet, son. Maybe the mayor will appoint a group to do that later," one of the men answered.

After drifting around town a little longer, Charlie decided to go home—or rather, to go where home was yesterday. He pictured Maggie there searching for him.

Having seen part of his house fall into the raging waters, he dreaded what he'd find when he got there. Reason told him the wind and flood had swept away the whole house, along with everything he and his mother and sister owned. But Charlie didn't know what else he could do except try to go home.

Chapter 11

Family

$\mathcal{E}$ xcept for a house here and there that had with-stood the storm, Charlie wouldn't have recognized the once familiar streets. He trudged through the foul-smelling slime, and frequently, he had to climb over an accumulation of rubble. Twice, he thought he heard cries for help from deep beneath piles of wreckage. He hoped rescue teams could save the people trapped there.

Charlie wondered if Thad and his family had lived through the hurricane. He could take Thad's street to get to his own home, so he chose that route.

When Charlie saw Thad's house, battered but still standing, his spirit soared. The front steps and porch had washed away, but a long board led from the ground up to the entrance. Charlie started yelling. "Thad! Thad! Mr. Brickel! Mrs. Brickel!" He walked up the plank, and called at the door, "Is anyone here?"

Thad came running from the back of the house and threw his arms around Charlie. This scared Joshua, and he cried. Charlie blushed as he quickly explained to Thad how he rescued the child and why he wore girls' clothing.

Thad smiled and patted Charlie on the shoulder. "I'm so happy to see you alive I don't care if you wear pink dresses from now on."

Charlie's stomach growled from hunger. He could tell Joshua needed to eat, too. While he talked to Thad, he sat down in the doorway and spooned the remainder of the milk into the baby's mouth.

"I've been trying to find Mama and Maggie," he said. "I don't know for sure they're alive, but I have a feeling they are. What about your family?"

"My mother and little brother are in the kitchen digging under the ruins—looking for something we can eat. The back of the house is in shambles, but Mama thinks she can find some food the storm didn't damage."

"Your father isn't here?" Charlie asked.

"He was working at our hardware store in town when the storm hit, and he never came home," Thad said, blinking back tears. "This morning, one of the men from the store told us Father left for home yesterday about four o'clock. We don't know what's happened to him."

"I'm sorry," Charlie told him. "But maybe he couldn't make it home and stayed some place else last night. A lot of men are in town trying to figure out how to handle all the wreckage—he may be with them. Don't give up on him yet."

Joshua burped and fell asleep on Charlie's shoulder.

"All my trouble to get him into dry clothes didn't do much good," Charlie told Thad. "He's wet again!"

"I never thought I'd see you tending to a baby," Thad teased with a half-smile.

"I learned how because I had to. We'll talk more later. I'm anxious—and scared at the same time—to get home and find out if Mama and Maggie are there."

He carefully made his way down the plank to the ground. He had walked away from the house when he heard Thad call. "My mother said to tell you that you—and your family if you find them—are welcome to stay with us should you need to."

"Thanks," Charlie yelled back. "I'll be in touch with you."

As Charlie neared what had been, only yesterday, the residential area where he lived, he didn't see a house. Nothing stood between him and the Gulf of Mexico but a tall heap of furniture, parts of boats, household goods, and wood from wrecked homes. The line of debris, about six blocks back from the beach, stretched along the coast as far as Charlie could see.

He knew most of the people he saw searching through rubbish for their belongings. He didn't stop to talk. He trudged on toward the site of his home. His heart beat harder. He tried to concentrate on rejoining Mama and Maggie, not on the destruction.

Charlie thought he recognized the spot where their house had stood. He paused a short distance away. He saw a woman bending over, digging through some litter—all that remained of his lifelong home. He stepped closer. The woman stood up. "Mama! Mama!" he called.

As they hugged each other, Charlie heard barking and felt Spatter jumping on his legs. He glanced down and dropped one hand to rub the dog's head.

"Oh, Charlie, you're safe," Mama cried. "I prayed you would be."

"Where's Maggie?" he asked. "She's all right, isn't she? I know she's been thinking about me."

"Yes, she's fine. I didn't know where to look for you, but Maggie begged me to come home. She said we'd find you here. She left a few minutes ago to ask others nearby if they had seen you. Whose baby is this?"

"I have his mother's name. I pulled him from the flood." Charlie looked down at the pink dress. "The storm tore my clothes off. This was all I could find to wear."

"Clothes aren't important—we're together." Mama patted him and touched his face. "The hurricane ripped our clothes off, too. A woman gave Maggie and me what we're wearing. My dress was so long, I tied this piece of rope around my waist to pull up the skirt. Now, tell me about saving the baby."

Before Charlie could answer, he heard Maggie screaming, and he saw her running toward them. "I knew you were alive," she squealed. "And I knew you'd come here."

"This time, I think we read each other's minds," he said.

As Charlie and Maggie hugged, Maggie asked, "Why are you dressed like a girl? And where did you get this baby?"

Charlie explained. "While we floated together on the overturned porch, I saw a cradle and heard crying. I didn't have time to tell anyone what I was about to do. I knew I had to act fast or the baby would drown.

"I almost didn't make it—a piece of wood hit me on the head and stunned me for several seconds—but I got the baby, and we ended up spending the night in a tree. There were snakes—I milked a cow—I had no clothes, so I put on this dress."

"At first, I thought you'd been knocked off the raft, because I knew how you felt about water," Maggie told him. "With my head down, I didn't see you go in. But after a few minutes, I had a feeling you'd jumped in on purpose. I didn't know why, but the more I thought about it, the more certain I became it wasn't an accident."

Charlie laughed and nodded his head. "You were right again."

"Let me hold the baby," Maggie said. "Is it a boy or a girl?"

"He's a boy. His name is Joshua." Charlie carefully put the baby in Maggie's arms. "Be gentle with him, and you need to support his head."

Spatter yelped and jumped on Charlie's legs for attention. Charlie picked up the dog and loved on him. "Spatter stinks, but you're holding the wet one," he teased Maggie. "And before long, he'll be hungry again. I'll have to find more milk for him. He really lets you know when he wants to eat."

Mama and Maggie both smiled. "You've learned a lot about babies since yesterday," Mama said.

"Maybe so," Charlie said. "But I also learned something else—"

Maggie interrupted him. "Oh, Charlie, I see Aaron Yates and his brother headed this way. Hide before they see you in that dress."

Charlie's eyes narrowed. He lifted one eyebrow. His mouth formed a sly grin. "I'm not going to hide. Let them come on," he said.

As the two boys approached, Aaron called, "Mrs. Byrd, Billy and I are surveying the storm's damage. I'm happy to see you and your two daughters are alive and well."

As if considering each step, Charlie started slowly toward Aaron and Billy. "Where's Jared?" he asked.

"We don't know, Miss." Billy snickered.

Charlie bolted. When he reached the boys, he suddenly stuck out his hand to Aaron. "Let's shake and declare a truce. And you may borrow my dress any time you feel like wearing it," he said.

Charlie grinned at the startled looks on Aaron's and Billy's faces as they shook hands with him. Neither brother uttered a word. They turned and scurried away.

Maggie stared. Her mouth opened in a look of disbelief before she asked, "Mama, are you sure this is my brother, Charlie?"

"It's me all right," Charlie said. "Those two won't ever make me mad again."

"Charlie, I'm so proud of you," Mama told him. "You never had a bad temper until after your father's accident. And I've always thought, one of these days you'd learn to control it. Only, I never dreamed it would come about because of a hurricane."

Charlie grinned at his mother. "Maybe the wind blew it out of me and made me see what is really important."

"I've known all along, the things you got angry about weren't the real problem," Mama said. "For four years, you've had rage inside of you because of losing your father."

"I know," Charlie admitted. "I felt cheated—and I was mad—because the sea took my papa away from me. I even thought the sea wanted to get me, too."

"I can tell you're happy now, even though we don't have a home or clothes or anything to eat," Mama said.

"Well, we have each other," Charlie said. "A lot of people aren't so fortunate."

Maggie smiled. "And we have a baby to take care of, at least for a while. And we don't have to dread Charlie's temper!"

Chapter 12

The Stranger

When Charlie showed Mama and Maggie the note he'd found pinned inside the baby's diaper, Mama said, "I hope the mother, Mrs. Packard, survived. If we find out she didn't, I'll see about adopting little Joshua myself."

"Where's Uncle Elmo?" Charlie asked. "And I've wondered about Aunt Lily and Mr. and Mrs. Hill. I saw the women get hit by a board and knocked into the current."

"I'm fairly certain Uncle Elmo was killed, and I'm concerned about the others," Mama said. "I don't know how Aunt Lily and Mrs. Hill could have lived—when the water drove them underneath the debris. And I never saw Mr. Hill after he jumped from the window. But I've been praying that somehow they all came through it."

"I've seen a lot of people who got hurt but are still alive," Charlie said. "Maybe they made it, too. What happened to Uncle Elmo?"

"We rode the porch for about four hours," Mama said. "During that time, a piece of slate from a roof hit Uncle Elmo on the head. He collapsed. He lay unconscious and bleeding badly from the deep gash. I tried to hold him, but I couldn't fight the wind along with the erratic motion of the porch. He was thrown into the water."

"It took all the strength we had to keep ourselves on the porch," Maggie told Charlie. "When I saw Mama trying to hang onto Uncle Elmo, I thought both of them would fall off."

Mama nodded. "I don't think Maggie and I could have lasted much longer, if the porch hadn't lodged against a tall pile of debris. We saw a two-story house, so we crept along about a hundred yards of wood and refuse to reach the second floor."

"We were exhausted, but some people inside helped us crawl through a window," Maggie said.

"The owners welcomed us and gave us food and these clothes," Mama told him. "More people piled up against the same wreckage and took shelter in the home. By morning, it was crowded, so we thanked the owners and left to look for you."

"And even Spatter made it," Charlie said, as he rubbed the dog's ears.

"Only because Maggie lay on top of him throughout our wild ride on the porch," Mama said.

"Give Spatter a little credit, too," Maggie insisted. "He managed on his own when we crossed the big pile of trash to get to the house. He crouched low and followed us."

Charlie patted Spatter's head. "You're a smart dog, aren't you?"

"We haven't found any trace of Breeze, though," Maggie said. "I still hope he will turn up."

Maggie held Joshua while Mama and Charlie sifted through the trash for any belongings they might salvage. "I had hoped to find our family Bible, but I don't recognize anything here," Mama said. She picked up the biggest man's nightshirt Charlie had ever seen.

"The wind and water carried everything away," Charlie said.

"I guess I really didn't expect to find any of our things, but I had to look," Mama told him.

"Here's a pair of someone's pants I think I can wear."

"No, Charlie. I know you want to get out of that dress, but those pants are coated with slimy mud. After awhile, we'll walk to town and find out what we should do to get food and clothing."

"I do feel foolish in this outfit. But with all that's happened, feeling foolish is something to laugh about."

Joshua began to fret. "We need to look for some milk. He's hungry," Maggie said.

Charlie took Joshua. "I'll go. I want to check on Thad's father, anyway."

Later, Charlie and Spatter sat with Thad while Charlie fed Joshua. He got the milk from one of Thad's neighbors whose cow had lived through the storm.

"Thank you for the shirt and pants," Charlie said.

"The pants are too big for you, but they look a heap better than that pink dress." Grinning, Thad stood up and, with his arms out at his sides, pretended to hold up a long skirt. Charlie laughed.

"If I hadn't been so worried about my father, I would have thought to give you some clothes earlier," Thad told him.

"I'm glad he's all right," Charlie said. "How did you find out?"

"After you left, he came home looking for us. But he has gone back to town for a meeting with the mayor."

The sun shone directly overhead as Charlie left carrying the sleeping baby and a bundle containing a wedge of cheese, some chipped beef, and two pears. Thad's mother had tied the food up in a piece of cloth. Spatter walked beside Charlie in the gray mud.

"Hello! You there with the baby—wait!" a man yelled.

Charlie put his arm up to shade his eyes, so he could see who called to him. About a block away, the man, wearing torn and muddy clothes, began to wave his hands and run in Charlie's direction.

Charlie gasped. A big lump rose in his throat. It was the bearded stranger who had watched their house! Why did the man now want to talk to him? Charlie walked faster.

Spatter sounded his "greeting" bark and bounded off toward the man.

"Spatter, come back," Charlie shouted. Spatter didn't stop.

"Wait! You have something I want," the man yelled, as he hurried to catch up with Charlie.

Charlie thought the man must want the baby, so he tried to run. The slimy muck and clumps of seaweed on the ground grabbed his feet with each step.

"Boy, stop! You did something to me—I have to talk to you," the man said.

Charlie stopped. He turned to face the stranger. *I believe it's me he wants, not Joshua. He must be mad because Thad and I tried to catch him with a rope. Well, it's time I find out who he is and put an end to this mystery.*

With Spatter by his side, the man caught up to Charlie. This time, Charlie didn't duck his head. He looked directly into the dark brown eyes that had scared him at the Midway. Why were the eyes so familiar?

Charlie stood up straight and held his shoulders back. "I don't mean to be disrespectful, but I need some answers," he demanded in a voice as deep as he could muster.

"Please wait! You did something to me," the man said again. "You caused me to begin to remember. So, first, *I* need an answer from *you*. Are you Charlie Byrd?"

Charlie glared at the man. A memory buried deep inside him nudged his brain. Then the truth hit him as unexpectedly as when a hidden grass burr attacks a bare foot. He didn't understand, yet he recognized, not only the eyes, but the *voice* of his father as well.

"Papa C? How can it be you?" he asked.

Tears wet Papa C's eyes, as he put his arms around Charlie. Charlie held the baby in one arm, but he held his other arm stiffly by his side. When his father hugged him, Charlie pulled away and stepped back.

"Where have you been?" Charlie asked. "Why did you do this to us? You've been alive all along!"

"I can explain. But first, is your mother all right? And Maggie?"

"Yes. They both survived. They're not far from here—where our house used to be. But I wonder if Mama will even want to see you after you left us for four years."

Joshua began to cry. "Whose baby is this?" Papa C asked.

"I rescued him from the storm," Charlie said. He wiped his hand on the borrowed pants he wore and stuck one of his fingers into the baby's mouth. Joshua sucked on it and got quiet.

"Why did you leave? And why didn't you tell me who you were when you came back?" Charlie asked.

"Let's go on. I can't wait to see the others. We can talk as we walk. I didn't intend to leave you. You might say I've been lost. That day, four years ago, a squall came up and we couldn't make it back to shore. The boat capsized. I never saw my friends again. I was tossed about in the Gulf, and part of the boat hit me on the head."

"We thought you drowned that day you went fishing," Charlie said.

"Until yesterday, I could only remember some men on a fishing boat hauling me from the water. They dressed the wound on my head and took me back to Freeport with them."

"Didn't you know who you were?"

"No, I didn't know my name or where I lived. I had forgotten everything that happened before the accident. I stayed around Freeport for about a month trying to discover who I was. Try as I might, I couldn't recall anything about my life.

"I saw the initials, *CB*, embroidered on a handkerchief I found in my pocket, so I gave myself the name of Clay Ballard. I moved to Houston and got a job working in a warehouse. The doctors in Houston said the blow on my head—and the shock from struggling in the water for hours—had caused me to forget everything. They assured me, at some point in my life I would start to remember.

113

They said, most likely, a person or circumstance would jar my memory, and it would return."

"Why did you come to Galveston?" Charlie asked.

"At the beginning of the summer, some of the men I work with asked me to take a trip to Galveston with them. I did, and the city seemed familiar. After that first time, I often visited Galveston on weekends. I felt drawn to a particular house here, but I didn't know why. Now I do. I was trying to go home."

"You look so different," Charlie said. "You've lost weight, and you have a beard and mustache. I didn't recognize you, but every time I saw you, I got an odd feeling inside. It scared me. Some part of me must have known you."

Papa C nodded he understood. "Yesterday, when I saw you at the Midway, I realized I should know *you*. So I tried as hard as I could to figure out what part you had played in my life."

"Did you remember me?" Charlie asked.

"Not fully, until the hurricane hit. But seeing you at the Midway, along with a turbulent sea, must have jarred my memory. During the storm, I rode a section of a roof for about five hours. As the waves tossed me about, I relived the boat accident. I was even hit on the head again by a flying board," Papa C said.

"During those hours I spent on the rooftop, I slowly recalled everything I'd forgotten. When the storm blew itself out early this morning, the ebbing tide left me beached miles away. But I began to search for the loving family I finally remembered. I went into the city. I looked all over. I was on my way to our home when I saw you."

Charlie still carried Joshua in one arm. With his free arm, he grabbed his father around the waist and hugged him hard. After heaving a long sigh, he said, "That terrible hurricane destroyed our house—our whole city—and killed many people, but it did one good thing. It brought you back."

"Charlie, it's sad so many people lost loved ones, because they can never be replaced. But the city of Galveston will come back. I'm sure of it. I thank God my family survived, and I'm eager to see your mother and Maggie. Let's hurry!"

"We're almost there," Charlie said. "Now we can really go home!"

Boys standing on a pipe used to pump in sand
for grade raising.

(Above):
Children playing in the sand and salt water
during grade raising.
(Below):
House placed on stilts in preparation for grade raising.

(Above and Below):
House before and after sand was pumped under it.

Building of the Galveston seawall (1902–1904).
Pouring cement into a form.

People enjoyed strolling along the seawall and on the beach.
The granite boulders provided them with a place to sit.
This picture was taken about 1905.

The Rebuilding
of Galveston

*I*n terms of lives lost, the hurricane that devastated Galveston on September 8, 1900, is still considered the worst natural disaster in the history of the United States. No one knows exactly how many people the storm killed, but most authorities place the number at approximately 6,000.

Before the storm, people in Galveston had talked of building a seawall, a concrete barrier to hold back the sea. They didn't build it because it cost too much money.

After the hurricane, some people wanted all the survivors of the killer storm to leave their wrecked homes and abandon the island. They favored locating the city on the mainland in a more protected spot. Fearing future storms, a few people did move away. But most of Galveston's residents stayed. They didn't see themselves as the type of folks to let a hurricane get the best of them.

Business and civic leaders believed Galveston would rise again if they could protect it from the sea. They knew the island must have a wall to prevent high water in the Gulf from flooding it. The people banded together to find a way to rebuild and save the city they loved.

A committee of civic leaders and local citizens appointed a board of engineers to draft plans for the protection of the new city. In 1902, the engineers recommended Galveston build a seawall and also raise the grade of the island. Since the water reached about 15 feet at its highest point during the 1900 storm, the engineers said to build the seawall 17 feet high.

The city and county found ways to pay for the work. The construction of the original concrete and steel seawall began in 1902 and was completed in 1904. Through the years, this first section has been extended both east and west.

To accomplish the second step in the plan, to raise the level of the city, great amounts of sand would have to be pumped onto the island. Many contractors thought this was next to impossible, but the men in charge of the city said it must be done. They asked for bids—for companies who wanted to do the work to say how much they would charge.

American firms refused to bid on the project. A German firm got the job. They brought four seagoing dredges from Germany to Galveston, and the work began. From the top of the seawall to Broadway Boulevard required filling to 17 feet. From Broadway north, the city had to be raised to a level of 10 feet.

The contractors dug a canal 200 feet wide and 20 feet deep. It led from the Gulf of Mexico to the interior of the island. The canal made it possible for the dredges to bring the filling material from the floor of the Gulf into the city.

Citizens who lived where the company built the canal agreed to the removal of their homes to vacant lots. Upon completion of the work, an American dredging company filled in the canal, and many people moved their houses back to their original locations.

Crews of workers built dikes around one section of the town at a time. They lifted up everything in that area so the sand could be poured underneath. Property owners paid for raising their own structures.

Huge buildings, such as St. Patrick's Catholic Church weighing 3,000 tons and Grace Episcopal Church at 400 tons, were placed on jacks. Streetcar tracks, water and sewer mains, and gas lines had to be lifted. Workers set homes and schools on stilts. The people continued to live in their homes while dredges pumped murky sand under them. The sand buried plants and shrubs. Residents had to walk on narrow planks. Galveston became known as a "city on stilts," but business, school, and church services went on as usual.

The German dredges took on their cargo of sand and water from the bottom of the Gulf. Then they traveled up the canal and discharged their load through large pipes onto the land. To their mothers' dismay, many youngsters played in the mud, sometimes even as it came shooting out of the pipes.

After awhile, the water ran from the filled areas into drainage ditches dug for that purpose. But when the sand dried completely, the island had another problem. The wind swept sand everywhere, so the people spent more money to cover the sand with topsoil from the mainland. The city rebuilt covered-up streets and sidewalks, and citizens replanted trees, shrubs, and flowers.

The German firm finished their contract for raising the island in 1910. During that time and in years since, American dredging companies added filling material to other areas.

The residents' inconvenience and expense paid off first in August of 1915, when another severe hurricane hit Galveston. This storm caused only slight damage.

Due to the seawall and the raising of the island, the city of Galveston has continued to grow. Today, once again, it is a popular seaside resort with a busy port and large businesses.

Sandy beaches, fine restaurants and hotels, museums, quaint shops in the restored Strand district, old mansions to tour, the scenic Seawall Boulevard, Moody Gardens, an abundance of beautiful oleanders, and many other attractions bring thousands of tourists to the island.

Acknowledgments

Personal interview in 1991 in Houston with 103-year-old Jennie Karbowski and her daughter, Sheppard Aurich. When Mrs. Karbowski was twelve, she lived in Galveston. She and her immediate family survived the hurricane. Her brother got separated from the others, but the next day they found him wearing a dress.

The Galveston Storm of 1900, a master's thesis by Frank Thomas Harrowing (University of Houston, 1950). After writing his master's thesis, Mr. Harrowing continued to study the hurricane of 1900. He is considered to be an authority on this storm. I wish to thank him for giving me a personal interview and then graciously consenting to read my story for accuracy.

The Galveston Daily News, especially issues published in 1900, housed in the Rosenberg Library, Galveston, Texas.

Articles and photographs in the Galveston and Texas History Department of the Rosenberg Library, Galveston, Texas.

Galveston in 1900, by Clarence Ousley, William C. Chase, 1900, Atlanta, Georgia.

A Weekend in September, by John Edward Weems, Texas A&M University Press, 1957, College Station and London.

Death from the Sea, by Herbert Molloy Mason, Dial Press, 1972, New York, New York.

Galveston, A History, by David G. McComb, University of Texas Press, 1986, Austin, Texas.

The cover photograph and all other photographs are courtesy of the Rosenberg Library, Galveston, Texas.